I0606941

James Hervey Simpson

Coronado's March in Search of the Seven Cities of Cibola

and discussion of their probable location

James Hervey Simpson

Coronado's March in Search of the Seven Cities of Cibola
and discussion of their probable location

ISBN/EAN: 9783337405663

Printed in Europe, USA, Canada, Australia, Japan

Cover: Foto ©Andreas Hilbeck / pixelio.de

More available books at **www.hansebooks.com**

CORONADO'S MARCH

WASHINGTON:
GOVERNMENT PRINTING OFFICE.
1871.

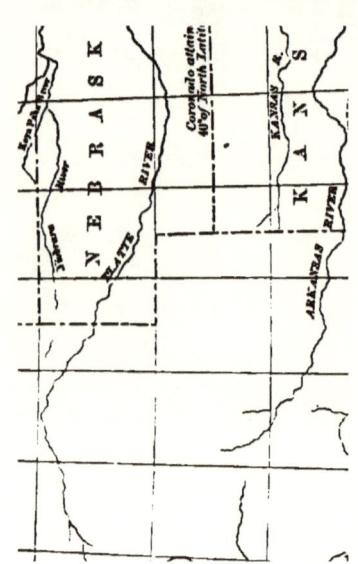

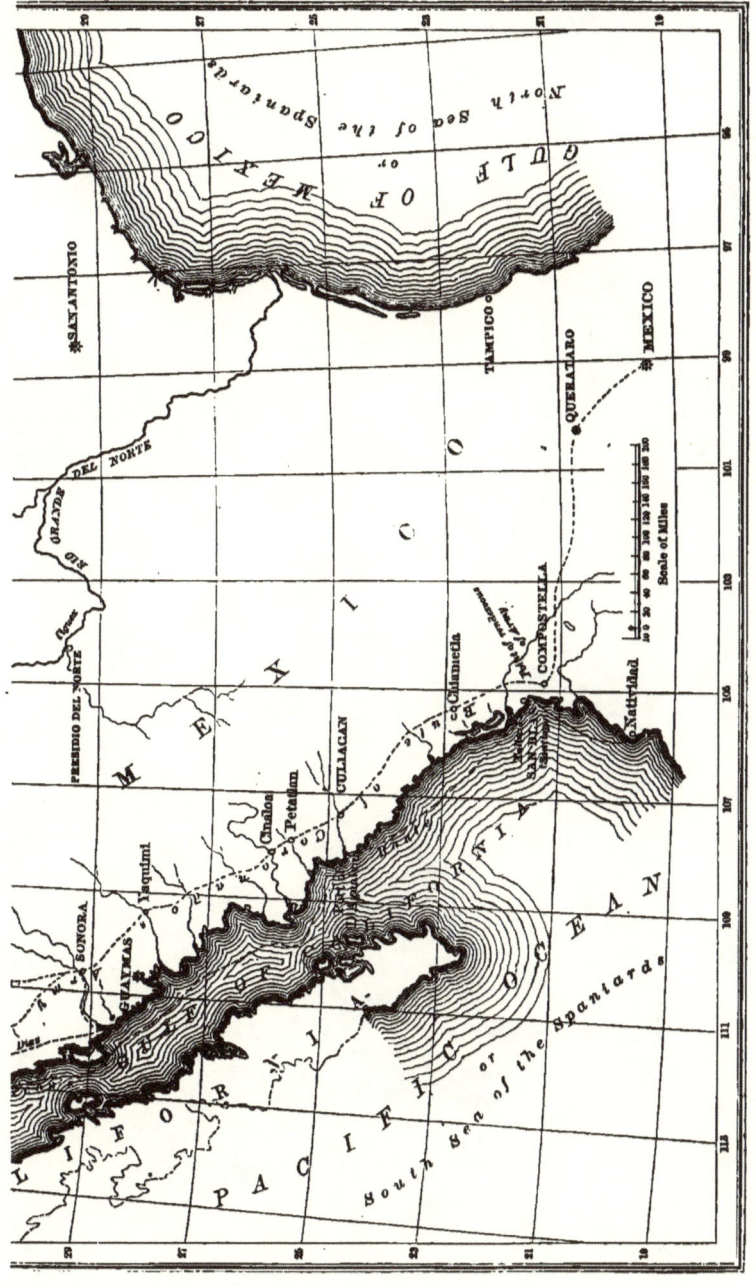

CORONADO'S MARCH IN SEARCH OF THE "SEVEN CITIES OF CIBOLA" AND DISCUSSION OF THEIR PROBABLE LOCATION.

By Brevet Brigadier General J. H. SIMPSON, *Colonel of Engineers, U. S. A.*

The early Spanish explorations in Mexico in search of the " seven cities of Cibola " have always been of great interest to students of American history. Recent publications have drawn my attention anew to the vast geographical field embraced in the toilsome march of Vasquez de Coronado and his adventurous followers, and, having in years past been engaged officially in the United States service in exploring that remote region, I have been tempted to reinvestigate the grand enterprise of the Mexican government in 1540, and venture to offer the following essay as an expression of my well-considered views, derived, in early life, from observation of the field itself, and confirmed by careful study of all the authorities within my reach. Besides this, friends, in whose opinion I trust, believe that my reconnoissances of a large part of the country traversed by Coronado and his followers give me some advantages in the discussion of this subject over other investigators, who have not been favored by personal inspection and scientific location of the important points embraced in the adventurers' march, so that I now submit my conclusions with less diffidence than I should have done had I not received in advance their cordial encouragement.

I must acknowledge my indebtedness to the library of the Peabody Institute of this city, to the library of the Historical Society of Maryland, and to the private library of the president of this last-mentioned society, Colonel Brantz Mayer, all of which have been thrown open to me in my researches. I must also express my particular obligations to Colonel Mayer for the very valuable aid he has afforded me in the preparation of this article, by the use of his excellent translation (yet in manuscript) of Ternaux Compans' version of the " Relation du Voyage de Cibola," entrepris en 1540, par Pédro de Castañeda de Nagera," published in Paris in 1838.

The arrangement of the following essay is, first, a brief narrative of the march of Coronado from the city of Mexico to the " seven cities of Cibola" and the province of Quivira, together with an account of the expeditions of his subordinate officers, naval and military; and second, the discussion of the subject of the location of the important places visited in the several expeditions; and, in order to a clear understanding of the text, I accompany it with a map, for which, under my direction as to details of route, I am indebted to Mr. N. H. Hutton, civil engineer, whose knowledge of New Mexico and Arizona, derived from his association with Generals Whipple and Parke, as assistant engineer, in their explorations in New Mexico and Arizona in 1853–'56, has been of material service to me.

In the year 1530, Nuño de Guzman, president of New Spain, was informed by his slave, an Indian, from the province of Tejos, situated somewhere north from Mexico, that in his travels he had seen cities so large that they might compare with the city of Mexico; that these

cities were seven in number, and had streets which were exclusively oc-
cupied by workers in gold and silver; that to reach them a journey
of forty days through a desert was required; and that travelers penetrated the interior of that region by directing their steps northwardly
between the two seas.

Nuño de Guzman, confidently relying on this information, organized
an army of four hundred Spaniards and twenty thousand Indian allies
of New Spain,* and set out in search of these seven wonderful cities;
but, after reaching the province of Culiacan, he encountered such great
difficulties on account of the mountains he had to cross that he abandoned the enterprise, and contented himself with colonizing the province of Culiacan.

In the mean time, the Tejos Indian who had been his guide dying, the
seven cities remained only known by name, till about eight years afterward, when there arrived in Mexico three Spaniards named Alvar
Nuñez Cabeça de Vaca, Andrès Dorantes, and Alonso del Castillo
Maldonado, accompanied by an Arabian negro named Estevanico, (Stephen.)† These persons had been wrecked with the fleet which Pam-

---

* Castañeda's Relations, Ternaux Compans' Collections, Paris, 1838, p. 2. Hakluyt,
quoting from a letter written by the Viceroy Antonio de Mendoça to the Emperor
Charles V, says: "Nuño de Guzman departed out of the city of Mexico with 400
horsemen and 14,000 Indians." (Hakluyt's Voyages, vol. iii, p. 436, new ed. London,
1810.) .

† This is according to Castañeda's account; but according to that of Cabeça de Vaca,
Ternaux Compans' Collections, these persons arrived in New Spain in 1536, or six instead of eight years after Nuño de Guzman's expedition. Their adventures were so
remarkable I cannot refrain from saying something about them:
Pamphilo de Narvaez sailed from the West Indies early in 1528, with four hundred
men, eighty horses, and four ships, for the purpose of exploring the country of Florida,
of which he had been made governor. He seems to have reached the harbor of Santa
Cruz (supposed to be Tampa Bay) in April of that year, and on the 1st May debarked
with three hundred men, forty of whom were mounted, for the purpose of exploring
the interior of the country. His course was northwardly, and generally parallel to
the coast. On the 26th June he reached an Indian town called *Apalache*, where he
tarried twenty-five days. He then journeyed in nine days to a place called Aute.
Continuing his course thence westwardly for several days, his men became so dispirited
from finding no gold, and on account of the rough treatment of the natives, that they
returned to Aute, where, hearing nothing of their ships, which had been ordered to
coast along with them and await their arrival at some good harbor, they constructed
five small boats, in which two hundred and fifty of the party (all who had not died or
been killed by the natives) embarked, steering along the coast westwardly for Panuco,
on the coast of Mexico. At length they reached the mouth of a river, the current of
which was so strong as to prevent their making headway against it, and whose fresh
water was carried out some distance into the gulf. About seven days after, while making
their way with great difficulty westwardly, the boat commanded by Cabeça de Vaca
was cast on an island, called by them Malhado, (Misfortune.) A day or two after this
·Cabeça de Vaca's boat and all the others were capsized in a storm off the island of
Malhado, except that of the governor of Narvaez, which seems to have drifted out
to sea, and, with its crew, was never afterward heard of. Those of the party that
were not drowned remained on the island of Malhado and main land adjacent for six
years, and endured from the Indians, who had enslaved them, the greatest indignities.
From this cause, and from starvation and cold, the greater portion of them died. At
length four of them, (those mentioned in the text above,) all that probably survived,
escaped from their bondage, taking in their flight a northern course, toward the
mountains, probably, of Northern Alabama. Thence their course was westwardly
across the Mississippi (which was doubtless "the great river coming from the North,"
spoken of by Cabeça) and Arkansas rivers, to the headwaters of the Canadian, which
they seem to have crossed just above the great cañon of that river, (where Coronado
crossed it in his outward route to Quivira, of which more in the sequel;) thence
southwestwardly through what is now New Mexico and Arizona to Culiacan, in Old
Mexico, near the Pacific Coast, which they reached in the spring of 1536. (See narrative of Alvar Nuñez Cabeça de Vaca, translated by Buckingham Smith, Washington,
1851; and, in confirmation of the above specified crossing of the Canadian River,
"The Relations of Castañeda, by Ternaux Compans," p. 120.)
Mr. Albert Gallatin, in his essay, vol. 2, pp. 56, 57, Transactions of American Ethno-

philo de Narvaez had conducted to Florida, and after crossing the
country from one sea to the other had reached Mexico.

The tales they told were quite marvelous. They stated to the then
viceroy, Don Antonio de Mendoça, that they had carefully observed the
country through which they had passed, and had been told of great and
powerful cities, containing houses of four or five stories, &c. The viceroy communicating these declarations to the new governor, Francisco
Vasquez de Coronado, the latter set out with haste to the province of
Culiacan, taking with him three Franciscan friars, one of whom, by
name Marcos de Niça, in the language of the chronicler Castañeda, was
theologian and priest. As soon as he reached Culiacan he dispatched
the three Franciscans, with the negro Stephen before mentioned, on a
journey of discovery, with orders to return and report to him all they
could ascertain by personal observation of the seven celebrated cities.
The monks, not being well pleased with the negro on account of his
excessive avarice, sent him in advance to pacify the Indians through
whose country he had previously passed, and to prepare the way for the
successful prosecution of their journey. Stephen, as soon as he reached
the country of the "seven cities of Cibola," demanded, as Castañeda
says, not only their wealth but their women.

The inhabitants not relishing this killed him and sent back all the
others that had accompanied him, except the youths, whom they retained.
The former, flying to their homes, encountered the monks before mentioned, in the desert sixty leagues from Cibola.* When the holy fathers
heard the sorrowful intelligence of the death of Stephen, they became
so greatly alarmed that, no longer trusting even the Indians who had
accompanied the negro, they gave them all they possessed except the
ornaments used in the celebration of the mass, and forthwith returned,
by double-days' journey, without knowing more of the country than the
Indians had told them. The monks returning to Culiacan, reported
the results of their attempted journey to Coronado, and gave
him such a glowing description of all the negro had discovered and of
what the Indians had told them, "as well as of the islands filled with
treasure, which they were assured existed in the Southern sea,"† that he
decided to depart immediately for Mexico, taking with him Friar Marcos de Niça, in order that he might narrate all he had seen to the viceroy. He also magnified the importance of the discovery by disclosing
it only to his nearest friends, and by pledging them to secrecy.

Arrived at Mexico, he had an interview with the viceroy, and proclaimed everywhere that he had found "the seven cities" searched for
by Nuño de Guzman, and busied himself with preparing an expedition
for their conquest. Friar Marcos having been made, through the influence of the monks, the provincial of the Franciscans, their pulpits re-

logical Society, states that the river referred to above, whose current was so strong
and which Narvaez's party could not stem, was the Mississippi; but this is not the view
of Mr. Smith, who has laid down the routes of Narvaez and party as extending no
further west than *Leaf River*, which lies to the eastward of the Mississippi River. His
idea, however, that the island of Santa Rosa, at the mouth of Pensacola Bay, was
Malhado, I think erroneous, for the reason that Cabeça de Vaca expressly says this
island was "half a league broad and five leagues (or seventeen miles) long," whereas
Santa Rosa Island, according to the maps, is as much as forty-seven miles long. It is
possible, however, that by accretions the island may have attained this length since
Cabeça de Vaca was wrecked upon it.

* So says Castañeda; but Marcos de Niça, in his account of his journey, distinctly
states that he approached so near the city of Cibola that from a high elevation he could
see the houses, and gives quite a particular description of them. (Relation of Friar
Marcos de Niça, Ternaux Compans' Collections, p. 279.)

† Castañeda's Relations, Ternaux Compans, p. 16.

sounded with the marvels of discoveries to such an extent that in a few days three hundred Spaniards and eight hundred Indians were assembled for the enterprise. Among the former were a great many gentlemen of good family, and probably there never had been an expedition in which there was such a large proportion of persons of noble birth. Francisco Vasquez de Coronado, the governor of New Galicia, was proclaimed captain general, because he was the author of the discovery, and the Viceroy Mêndoça did all he could to foster the enterprise.

Believing that if the army marched from the city of Mexico in a body the Indian allies would probably suffer, the viceroy appointed the town ·of Compostella, capital of New Galicia, one hundred and ten leagues from Mexico, as the place, and Shrove Tuesday, 1540,* the time of rendezvous. The troops having left Mexico, he ordered Don Pedro d'Alarcon to depart for La Nativitad, on the coast of the "Southern Sea," and with two vessels to go to Jalisco to take the supplies which the soldiers could not transport. After performing that duty he was to follow the march of the army along the coast, for it was believed, according to the then received accounts, that the army would never be distant from the vessels, and would always be in easy communication with them by means of the rivers.†

All these dispositions having been made, the viceroy departed for Compostella with a large body of gentlefolks. Everywhere he was received with great *éclat*, and when he reached Compostella he found the army well lodged and entertained by Christoval d'Onate, captain general of that country.

He reviewed the troops, by whom he was received with great rejoicing, and the next day after mass harangued them. He told them of their duties and of the advantageous result that this conquest would produce, not only on their fortunes, but by the conversion of the nations they would conquer, as well as for the service of his Majesty, who on his side promised them his bounty and additional favors. Finally he caused every one to be sworn on a missal containing the Holy Evangels not to abandon their general and to obey all his commands.

The next day the army with banners flying took up the line of march. For two days the viceroy accompanied it, and then returned to Mexico. No sooner, however, had the viceroy left the army than it began to experience all the hardships incident to a wild, mountainous country. The baggage had to be transported on horses, and, as many soldiers had never been accustomed to load them, they made sorry work of it. The consequence was that a great deal of their baggage was abandoned, and in order to get along at all many,a gentleman had to become a muleteer, and they who shirked from this necessary labor were regarded by their companions as lacking spifit.

Coronado arriving at Chiametta with his army, met at that point Captains Melchior Diaz and Juan de Saldibar, who with a dozen resolute men, by Coronado's orders, had explored the country as far as Chichilticale, which is on the border of the desert and two hundred leagues from Culiacan.‡ These officers gave in secret to the general such a dole-

---

* Castañeda's Relations, Ternaux Compans, p. 24. Castañeda says 1541, but, as Ternaux Compans has remarked in a note, he evidently must have made a mistake, for the letter of the viceroy to the Emperor Charles V, reporting the organization and progress of the expedition, bears date April 17, 1540.

† According to "Los Tres Siglos de Mexico, tom. I, Mexico, 1836," p. 129, "Mendoça dispatched Alarcon, with two ships, to observe the coast as far as the 36th degree of latitude, with instructions to make frequent embarkations and to join the army at that height."

‡ Castañeda gives in one place two hundred leagues as the distance; and in another, two hundred and twenty leagues. See his Rel. Ternaux Compans' Col., pp. 12, 20.

ful account of the country they had passed through, that, it leaking out, many in the army began to lose heart; and it was only by Friar Marcos de Niça insisting upon it, that the country was a good one, and that they should not leave it with empty hands, that they were persuaded to continue the march.

The day after Easter, the army took up its march for Culiacan, at which place they were well received by the citizens and furnished with all necessary supplies. This was the last town inhabited by Spaniards, and, therefore, the last from which they could gather provisions, except from the Indians with whom they might meet in their further march. It is represented by Castañeda, as being two hundred and ten leagues from the city of Mexico.*

After resting a couple of weeks at Culiacan, Coronado led the advance of his army, consisting of fifty cavaliers, a few infantry, his particular friends, and the monks, leaving the rest of the army with orders to march a fortnight after, and to follow his path. As Castañeda, describing his progress, expresses it, " when the general had passed through all the inhabited region to Chichilticale, where the desert begins, and saw that there was nothing good, he could not repress his sadness, notwithstanding the marvels which were promised further on. No one save the Indians who accompanied the negro had seen them, and already on many occasions they had been caught in lies. He was especially afflicted to find this Chichilticale, of which so much had been boasted, to be a single, ruined, and roofless house, which at one time seemed to have been fortified. It was easy to see that this house, which was built of red earth, was the work of civilized people who had come from afar.

" On quitting this place they entered the desert. At the end of fifteen days they came within eight leagues of Cibola, on the banks of a river which they named *Vermejo*, in consequence of its red and troubled water. Mullets resembling those of Spain were found in it. It was there that the first Indians of the country were discovered; but when these saw the Spaniards they fled and gave the alarm. During the night of the succeeding day, when not more than two leagues from the village, some Indians who were concealed suddenly uttered such piercing cries that our soldiers became alarmed, notwithstanding they pretended not to regard it as a surprise; and there were even some who saddled their horses the wrong way, but these were men who belonged to the new levies. The best warriors mounted their horses and scoured the country. The Indians, who knew the land, escaped easily, and not one of them was taken. On the following day, in good order, we entered the inhabited country. Cibola was the first village we discovered; on beholding it the army broke forth with maledictions on Friar Marcos de Niça. God grant that he may feel none of them !

" Cibola is built on a rock; this village is so small that, in truth, there are many farms in New Spain that make a better appearance. It may contain two hundred warriors. The houses are built in three or four stories; they are small, not spacious, and have no courts, as a single court serves for a whole quarter. The inhabitants of the province were united there. It is composed of seven towns, some of which are larger and better fortified than Cibola. These Indians, ranged in good order, awaited us at some distance from the village. They were very loth to accept peace; when they were required to do so by our interpreters, they menaced us by their gestures. Shouting our war-cry of Sant Iago, we charged upon and quickly caused them to fly.

---

* Castañeda's Rel., Ternaux Compans' Col., p. 149.

"Nevertheless, it was necessary to get possession of Cibola, which was no easy achievement, for the road leading to it was both narrow and winding. The general was knocked down by the blow of a stone as he mounted in the assault, and he would have been slain had it not been for Garci Lopez de Cardenas and Hernando d'Alvarado, who threw themselves before him and received the blows of the stones which were designed for him and fell in large numbers; nevertheless, as it is impossible to resist the first impetuous charge of Spaniards, the village was gained in less than an hour. It was found filled with provisions which were much needed, and, in a short time the whole province was forced to accept peace."[*]

The main army, which had been left at Culiacan under the command of Don Tristan d'Arellano, followed Coronado as directed by him, every one marching on foot, with lance in hand and carrying supplies. All the horses were laden. Slowly and with much fatigue, after establishing and colonizing Sonora, and endeavoring to find the vessels under Alarcon already referred to, by descending the river, in which they failed, the army reached Cibola. Here they found quarters prepared for them and rejoiced in the reunion of the troops, with the exception of certain captains and soldiers who had been detached on explorations.

Meantime, Captain Melchior Diaz, who had been left at Sonora, placed himself at the head of twenty-five choice men, and under the lead of guides directed his steps towards the southwest in hopes of discovering the coasts. His course was probably down the Rio Sonora, and not finding the vessels there he doubtless marched northward, keeping as close to the coast as the rivers would permit him. After traveling about one hundred and fifty leagues[†] it appears he arrived in a country in which there was a large river, called Rio del Tizon, whose mouth was two leagues wide. Here the captain learned that the vessels under Alarcon had been on the sea-coast, at a distance of three days' journey from that place. In the language of Castañeda, "When he reached the spot that was indicated, and which was on the bank of the river more than fifteen leagues from its mouth, he found a tree on which was written 'Alarcon has come thus far; there are letters at the foot of this tree.' They dug and found the letters, which apprised them that Alarcon, after having waited a certain length of time at that spot, had returned to New Spain, and could not advance further because that sea was a gulf; that it turned around the Isle of the Marquis, which had been called the Isle of California, and that California was not an island, but a part of land forming the gulf."[‡]

It appears that after a good deal of difficulty and a threatened attack from the natives, the party crossed the Rio del Tizon, on rafts, some five or six days' travel higher up, and continued its journey along the coast. Quoting from Castañeda, "When the explorers had crossed the Rio del Tizon, they continued following the coast, which at that place turns toward the southeast, for this gulf penetrates the land directly toward the north, and the stream flows exactly toward the mouth from north to south."[§] No better description could be given of the relative position of the Gulf of California, with respect to the Rio Colorado flowing into it from the north, than the foregoing.

This expedition was terminated by the death of Melchior Diaz, which occurred in a very singular manner, as follows: "One day a greyhound belonging to a soldier attacked some sheep which the Spaniards were

* Castañeda's Relations, Ternaux Compans, pp. 40, 41, 42, 43.
† Castañeda's Relations, Ternaux Compans, p. 49.
‡ Castañeda's Relations, Ternaux Compans, pp. 50, 51.   § Ibid, p. 104.

driving with them to serve as food in case of need, when Captain Melchior Diaz threw his lance at the beast, in order to drive him off. Unfortunately the weapon stuck in the ground with the point uppermost, and as Diaz could not rein in his horse, who was at a gallop, quickly enough, it pierced his thigh through and through, and severed his bladder. The soldiers at once decided to retrace their steps, taking their wounded chief with them. The Indians, who were always in rebellion, did not cease attacking them. The captain lived about twenty days, during which he was borne along with the utmost difficulty. When, at length, he died, all his troops returned in good array, (to Sonora,) without the loss of a single man, and after traversing the most dangerous places."*

In this connection it may be interesting to give some account of Alarcon's discovery of the Rio Colorado. It will be recollected that he was ordered by the Viceroy Mendoça to follow the march of the army with his vessels along the coast of the Southern Sea, as the Pacific Ocean was then called. From his relation to the viceroy † I gather the following:

On the 9th of May, 1540, Fernando Alarcon put to sea from La Natividad, in command of two ships, the Saint Peter and the Saint Catherine. He put into the ports of Xalisco and Aguaival, (respectively the ports of Compostella and Culiacan,) and finding Coronado and his army gone from this last-mentioned place, he continued his course northwardly along the coast, taking with him the ship St. Gabriel, which he found there laden with supplies for the army. At length arriving towards the upper end of what was till then believed to be a strait separating an island from the main land, but which he discovered to be a gulf, (the Gulf of California,) he experienced great difficulty in navigating, even with his small boats; and there were some in the expedition, he remarks, who lost heart and were anxious to return, as did Captain Francisco de Ullva, with his vessels, in a former voyage of discovery. Alarcon, it seems, however, had the necessary pluck, and, agreeably to the orders of the Viceroy Mendoça, he was determined to make his explorations as thorough as possible. After incredible hardships he managed to get his vessels to the bottom of the gulf, ("au fond du gulfe.") Here he found a very great river, the current of which was so rapid, that they could scarcely stem it. Taking two shallops and leaving the others with the ships, and providing himself with some guns of small caliber, on the 26th of August, 1540, he commenced the ascent of the river by hauling the boats with ropes.‡ On his way he met a large number of Indians,

---

* Castañeda's Relations, Ternaux Compans, p. 105.

† Ternaux Compans' Coll., p. 299–348.

‡ The most reliable information in relation to the Colorado River will be found in the report of Lieutenant Ives's ascent of that stream in 1858. (Ex. Doc. No. —, 36th Congress, 1st session.)   *   *   *   *   *   *

"From his account the region at the mouth of the Colorado is a flat expanse of mud, and the channels that afford entrance from the gulf are shifting and changeable. For 30 miles above the mouth the navigation is rendered periodically dangerous by the strength and magnitude of the spring tides.

"Between the tide-water and Fort Yuma, which is 150 miles from the mouth, the principal obstructions are sand-bars, continually shifting, having in some places but two feet of water upon them. There are no rocks, but snags are numerous although not very dangerous.

"For 180 miles above Fort Yuma the navigation is similar. The river passes through several chains of hills and mountains, forming gorges or cañons, sometimes of a considerable size. In these there is generally a better channel than in the valley.

"In the next 100 miles gravelly bars are frequent, with many stretches of good river and although the bad places are worse, the channel is better than below. For the succeeding 50 miles there are many swift rapids. The river bed is of coarse gravel and sand, and there are some dangerous sunken rocks. The Black Cañon, which is 25 miles

who made signs to him to return down the river, but by good manage-
ment he so appeased them that he was enabled to reach a distance
above the mouth of the river, such that in two and a half days, on his
return to the ships, on account of the swiftness of the current, he made
the same distance he had in fifteen and a half days in ascending the
river. On this expedition he learned from the Indians he met, some
particulars of the death of the negro Stephen, before referred to, at
Cibola, and of there being white persons like themselves at that place,
who doubtless belonged to Coronado's army. Alarcon was, however,
unable to communicate with the army on account of the desert intervening between them, and the great distance they were apart.

Refitting all his shallops this time for a second voyage up the river,
he left its mouth on the 14th of September, but was no more successful
in this than in his former expedition in communicating with Coronado.
Having, therefore, reached as far up the river as he thought expedient,
he planted a cross at that point, and deposited at its foot some letters,
in the hope that some persons of Coronado's army, searching for news
of the vessels, might find them. These letters, it has already been stated,
were found by Melchior Diaz on the Rio del Tizon, called by Alarcon
the "Bon Guide," after the device of his lordship Don Antonio de Mendoça, and at the present day the Rio Colorado.

At the end of Alarcon's relation to the viceroy he reports that he
found the latitude, as given by the "patrons and pilots of the Marquis
del Valle," wrong by two degrees; that he had gone further by four degrees than they, and that he had ascended the river a distance of eighty-
five leagues.* This report of Alarcon's is very interesting from its great
particularity and the many incidents it gives of the expedition; it shows
also that he was fully equal to the trust committed to him, and that
no explorer could have done more to carry out the orders of the Viceroy
Mendoça.

We will now return to the army under Coronado, at Cibola. This
general immediately set to work to explore the adjacent country. Hearing there was a province in which there were seven towns similar to
those of Cibola, he dispatched hither Don Pédro de Tobar with seventeen horsemen, three or four soldiers, and Friar Juan de Padilla, a Franciscan, who had been a soldier in his youth, to explore it. "The rumor
had spread among its inhabitants that Cibola was captured by a very
ferocious race of people who bestrode horses that devoured men, and as
they knew nothing of horses, this information filled them with the greatest
astonishment."† They, however, made some show of resistance to the
invaders in their approach to their towns, but the Spaniards charging
upon them with vigor, many were killed, when the remainder fled to the
houses and sued for peace, offering, as an inducement, presents of cotton
stuff, tanned hides, flour, pine nuts, maize, native fowls, and some
turquoises.

These people informing the Spaniards of a great river on which there

_____

long, is now reached, and in it the rapids are numerous and difficult. Calville is some
six miles above the head of this cañon." (Letter of General A. A. Humphreys, Chief
of Corps of Engineers United States Army, to Secretary of War, June 24, 1868, in his
annual report for 1868, part 2, p. 1195.)

* Alarcon's orders from the Viceroy Mendoça, as before stated, in a note, were to
explore as high as the 36th degree of latitude. According to his own account of the
distance he went up the Rio del Tizon, (Colorado,) he must have explored as far as
about the 34th degree, and if he went no higher up than where Melchior Diaz found
the tree, at the foot of which were letters from Alarcon, showing that there was the
highest point to which he had attained, the highest latitude he reached must have been
only about the 33d degree.

† Castañeda's Relations, Ternaux Compans, p. 59.

were Indians living, who were very tall, a report of the same on his return to Cibola was made by Don Pedro de Tobar to Coronado, who sent out another party consisting of twelve men, under Don Garci-Lopez de Cardenas, to explore this river. It appears from Castañeda's Relations that the party passed through Tusayan again on its way to the river and obtained from its inhabitants the necessary supplies and guides.

After a journey of twenty days through a desert it seems they reached the river, whose banks were so high that, as Castañeda expresses it, "they thought themselves elevated three or four leagues in the air." For three days they marched along the banks of the river, hoping always to find a downward path to the water, which from their elevation did not seem more than a yard in width, but which according to the Indians' account was more than half a league broad. But their efforts to descend were all made in vain. Two or three days afterward, having approached a place where the descent appeared practicable, the captain, Melgosa Juan Galeras, and a soldier, who were the lightest men in the party, resolved to make the attempt. They descended until those who remained above lost sight of them. They returned in the afternoon declaring that they had encountered so many difficulties that they could not reach the bottom; for what appeared easy when beheld from aloft, was by means so when approached. They added 'that they compassed about one-third of the descent, and that from thence the river already seemed very wide, which confirmed what the Indians stated. They assured them that some rocks which were seen from on high, and did not appear to be scarcely as tall as a man, were in truth loftier than the tower of the cathedral of Seville.[*]

Castañeda, after describing the further progress of the exploring party, goes on to say: "The river was the Tizon (Colorado.) A spot was reached much nearer its source than the crossing of Melchior Diaz and his people (before referred to;) and it was afterward known that the Indians which have been spoken of were the same nation that Diaz saw. The Spaniards retraced their steps (to Cibola) and this expedition had no other result."[†]

During the march they met with a cascade falling from a rock. The guides said that the white crystals hanging around it were formed of salt. They gathered and carried away a quantity thereof, which was distributed at Cibola.[‡]

[*] For 300 miles the cut edges of the table land rise abruptly, often perpendicularly, from the water's edge, forming walls from 3,000 to 6,000 feet in height. This is the great cañon of the Colorado, the most magnificent gorge as well as the grandest geological section of which we have any knowledge.
Again, the cañon of the Colorado at the mouth of Grand River is but a portion of the stupendous chasm which its waters have cut in the strata of the table lands, and of which a general description has been given. At this point its walls have an altitude of over 3,000 feet above the Colorado, and the bed of the stream is about 1,200 feet above the level of the sea, or 500 feet higher than those in the Black Cañon. A few miles further east, where the surface of the table lands has an altitude of nearly 7,000 feet, the dimensions of the cañon become far more imposing, and its cliffs rise to the height of more than a mile above the river. (Report of Lieutenant Joseph C. Ives, Corps of Topographical Engineers United States Army, upon the Colorado River, 1857–'58, Senate Ex. Doc. 30th Congress, 1st session. Geology, chapter v, p. 42; Chapter vi, p. 54.)
[†] Castañeda's Relations, Ternaux Compans, p. 64.
[‡] Lieutenant Ives speaks of having found salt on the Flax River, which Cardenas, party undoubtedly crossed or followed:
"At noon to-day we came to the object of our search—a well-beaten Indian trial' running toward the north. Camp was pitched at the place where it strikes the Flax River, and it is the intention to make the second attempt to-morrow to penetrate the unexplored region. Near by are several salt springs, and scattered over the adjacent surface are crystals of excellent salt." (Report of Lieutenant Ives, p. 117.)

I have thus briefly. described the explorations which were made by Coronado and his captains, as far as Cibola, on the northern edge of the great desert northward of Chichilticale; the branch expedition of Melchior Diaz from Sonora northwestward to and around the head of the Gulf of California, after crossing the Tizon (Colorado,) in search of the vessels; the exploration of the river Tizon, by Alarcon, in boats for 'a distance of 85 Spanish leagues,* or about 290 miles, above its mouth; the expedition of Don Pedro de Tobar from Cibola to Tusayan, lying to the northwest of Cibola twenty-five leagues; and the exploration of Don Garci Lopez de Cardenas from Cibola through Tusayan westwardly to the deeply cañoned river Tizon. I shall now give in as few words as I can some account of Coronado's subsequent explorations to the eastward of Cibola.

While the discoveries above mentioned were being made, some Indians living seventy leagues towards the east, in a province called Cicuyé, arrived at Cibola. There was with them a Cacique, surname Bigotes (Mustaches) on account of his wearing these long appendages. They had heard of the Spaniards, and came to offer their services and their friendship. They offered gifts of tanned skins, shields, and helmets, which the general reciprocated by giving them necklaces of glass beads, and bells, which they had never before beheld. They informed him of cows, because one of these Indians had one painted on his body." Castañeda goes on to say, but "we would never have guessed it, from seeing the skins of these animals, for they are covered with a frizzled hair, which resembles wool;"† thus showing that they certainly were buffaloes.

The general ordered Captain Hernando d'Alvarado to take twenty men and to accompany these Indians, but to return in eighty days to render an account of what he might have seen. Alvarado. departed with them, and "five days after they arrived at a village named Acuco, built on a rock. The inhabitants, who are able to send about two hundred warriors into the field, are the most formidable brigands in the province. This village was very strongly built, inasmuch as it was reached by only one path, and was built upon a rock precipitous on all its other sides, and at such a height that the ball from an arquebuse could scarcely reach its summit. It was entered by a stairway cut by the hand of man, which began at the bottom of the declivitous rock and led up to the village. This stairway was of suitable width for the first two hundred steps, but after these there were a hundred more much narrower, and when the top was finally to be reached' it was necessary to scramble up the three last *toises* by placing the feet in holes scraped in the rock, and as the ascender could scarcely make the point of his toe enter them he was forced to cling to the precipice with his hands. On the summit there was a great arsenal of huge stones, which the defenders, without exposing themselves, could roll down on the assailants, so that no army, no matter what its strength might be, could force this passage. There was on the top a sufficient space of ground to cultivate and store a large supply of corn, as well as cisterns to contain water and snow."‡

The Indians here, as at Tusayan, traced lines on the ground, and forbade the Spaniards to pass over them; but seeing the latter disposed

---

* Common Spanish league equals 3.42 American miles. (United States Ordnance Manual.)

† Castañeda's Relations, Ternaux Compans, p. 68. "Il est ici la question des bisons, que l'auteur nomme toujours *vacas*. Je me servirai dorénavant du mot de bison." (Note by Ternaux Compans.)

‡ Castañeda's Relations, Ternaux Compans, pp. 68, 69, 70.

for an attack, they quickly sued for peace, and presented to their conquerors a supply of birds' bread, tanned deer-skins, pine-nuts, seeds, flour, and corn.

Three days' journey thence Captain Alvarado and party reached a province called Tiguex, where, on account of Bigotes, whom the inhabitants knew, they were received very kindly; and the captain was so well pleased with what he saw that he sent a messenger to Coronado inviting him to winter in that country, which pleased the general greatly, as it made him believe that his affairs were growing better.

Five days' journey thence, Alvarado reached Cicuyé, a village very strongly fortified, and whose houses had four stories. He reposed here with his party some days, when he fell in with an "Indian slave who was a native of the county adjacent to Florida, the interior of which Fernando de Soto had lately explored."[*]

This Indian, whom they called il Turco, (the Turk,) on account of his resemblance to the people of that nation, spoke of certain large towns, and of large stores of gold and silver in his country,[†] and also of the country of the bisons, (buffaloes.) Alvarado took him as a guide to the bison country, and after he had seen a few of them he returned to Tiguex to give an account of the news to Coronado.

In the order of events, Coronado, who had remained at Cibola with the main body of the army, hearing of a province composed of eight towns, took with him thirty of the most hardy of his men and set out to visit it on his way to Tiguex. In eight or eleven days (the narrative is here obscure) he reached this province, called Tutahaco, which appears to have been situated on the Rio de Tiguex, below the city of Tiguex, for Castañeda expressly states that he afterward ascended the river and visited the whole province until he arrived at Tiguex. The eight villages composing this province were not like those of Cibola, built of stone, but of earth. He also learned of other villages still further down the river.

"On his arrival at Tiguex, Coronado found Hernando d'Alvarado with the Turk, and was not a little pleased with the news they gave him. This Indian told him that in his country there was a river two leagues wide, in which fish as large as horses were found; that there were canoes with twenty oarsmen on each side, which were also propelled by sails; that the lords of the land were seated in their sterns upon a dais, while a large golden eagle was affixed to their prows. He added that the sovereign of this region took his *siesta* beneath a huge tree, to whose branches golden bells were hung, which were rung by the agitation of the summer breeze. He declared, moreover, that the commonest vessels were of sculptured silver; that the bowls, plates, and dishes were of gold. He called gold *acochis*. He was believed because he spoke with great assurance, and because when some trinkets of copper were shown him he smelt them, and said they were not gold. He knew gold and silver very well, and made no account of the other metals. The general sent Hernando d'Alvarado to Cicuyé to reclaim the golden bracelets which the Turk pretended had been taken from him when he was made prisoner. When Alvarado arrived there the inhabitants received him kindly, as they had done before, but they pos-

---

[*] Castañeda's Relations, Ternaux Compans, p. 72. The basin of the Mississippi River and tributaries, in former days, were included in Florida by the Spaniards. (See note, p. 90.)

[†] The country of Quivira, which Coronado, as will be seen in the sequel, visited, and which, being adjacent to Florida, as stated above, must have been situated in the country tributary to the Missouri or Mississippi, and not near the Rio Grande, as some commentators have supposed.

itively affirmed that they had no knowledge of the bracelets, and they assured him that the Turk was a great liar, who deceived him. Alvarado, seeing there was nothing else he could do, lured the chief, Bigotes, and the Cacique under his tent, and caused them to be chained. The inhabitants reproached the captain with being a man without faith or friendship, and launched a shower of arrows on him. Alvarado conducted these prisoners to Tiguex, where the general retained them more than six months."[*]

This affair seems to have been the beginning of Coronado's troubles with the Indians, which were subsequently increased by his exacting a large quantity of clothing, which he divided among his soldiers.

Two weeks after Coronado left Cibola for Tiguex, agreeably to his orders, the army under the command of Don Tristan d'Arellano took up its march from that place for Tiguex. The first day they reached the handsomest, and largest village in the province, where they lodged. "There they found houses of seven stories, which were seen nowhere else. These belonged to private individuals, and served as *fortresses.* They rise so far above the others that they have the appearance of towers. There are embrasures and loop-holes from which lances may be thrown and the place defended. As all these villages have no streets, all the roofs are flat, and common for all the inhabitants; it is therefore necessary to take possession, first of all, of those large houses which serve as defenses."[†]

The army passed near the great rock of Acuco, already described, where they were well received by the inhabitants of the city perched on its summit.

Finally it reached Tiguex, where it was well received and lodged. The good news given by the Turk cast their past fatigues into oblivion, though the whole province was found in open revolt, and not without cause, for on the preceding day the Spaniards had burnt a village; and we have already seen that the imprisonment of Bigotes and the Turk, and the exactions of clothing by Coronado, had also very greatly exasperated them. The result of all this was that the Indians generally revolted, as they said, on account of the bad faith of the Spaniards, and the latter retaliated by burning some of their villages, killing a large number of the natives, and at last laying siege to and capturing Tiguex. This siege lasted fifty days, and was terminated at the close of 1540.[‡]

After the siege the general dispatched a captain to Chia, which had sent in its submission. It was a large and populous village, four leagues west of the Tiguex River. Six other Spaniards went to Quirix, a province composed of seven villages. All these villages were at length tranquilized by the assiduous efforts of the Spaniards to regain the confidence which they had justly lost by their repeated breaches of faith; but no assurances that could be given to the twelve villages in the province of Tiguex would induce *them* to return to their homes so long as the Spaniards remained in the country; and no wonder, for no more barbarous treachery was ever shown to a submissive foe than had been shown to these Tiguecans by these faithless Spaniards.

So soon as the Tiguex River, (Rio Grande,) which had been frozen for four months, was sufficiently free from ice, the army took up its march on the 5th of May, 1541, to Quivira, in search of the gold and silver which

---

*Castañeda's Relations, Ternaux Compans, pp. 76, 77, 78.
†Castañeda's Relations, Ternaux Compans, p. 80.
‡Castañeda says 1542, evidently an error, as may be ascertained by accounting for the time consumed by the army in its march from Chiametla, which it left on the next day after Easter, 1540. (See ante, p. 12.)

the Turk had said could be found there. Its route was via Cicuyé, twenty-five leagues distant. The fourth day after leaving Cicuyé and crossing some mountains it reached a large and very deep river, which passed pretty near to Cicuyé, and was therefore called the Rio de Cicuyé. Here it was delayed four days to build a bridge. Ten days after, on their march, they discovered some tents of tanned buffalo skins, inhabited by Indians who were like Arabs, and who were called Querechaos; continuing their march in a northeastwardly direction they soon came to a village in which Cabeça de Vaca and Dorantes (mentioned in the first part of this paper) had passed through on their way from Florida to Mexico.* The army met with and killed an incredible number of buffalo,† and after reaching a point 250 leagues (850 miles) from Tiguex, the provision giving out, Coronado, with thirty horsemen and six foot-soldiers, continued his march in search of Quivira, while the rest of the army returned to Tiguex under the command of Don Tristan d'Arellano. The narrative goes on to say : " The guides conducted the general to Quivira in forty-eight days, for they had traveled too much in the direc- tion of Florida. At Quivira they found neither gold nor silver, and learning from the Turk that he had, at the instance of the people of Cicuyé, purposely decoyed the army far into the plains to kill the horses, and thus make the men helpless and fall an easy prey to the natives, and that all he had said about the great quantity of silver and gold to be found there was false, they strangled him. The Indians of this region, so far from having large quantities of gold and silver, did not even know these metals. The Cacique wore on his breast a copper plate, of which he made a great parade, which he would not have done had he known anything about those precious metals. The army, as stated above, retreated to Tiguex before reaching Quivira. They took as guides some Teyans, through whose country they were passing, and were led back by a much more direct way than that they pursued in coming. These Teyans were a nomadic nation, and being constantly in the pursuit of game knew the country perfectly." It is narrated they guided the army thus : Every morning they watched to note where the sun rose, and directed their way by shooting an arrow in advance, and then before reaching this arrow they discharged another; in this way they marked the whole of their route to the spot where water was to be found, and where they encamped. "The army consumed only twenty-

---

* It will be recollected that it was on information given by these persons and two others, Maldonado and the negro Estevan, that this expedition was founded. (See ante p. 310.)

† The following minute and graphic description of the buffalo, seen by Coronado and his army, is taken from Gomara, as quoted in Hakluyt's Voyages, vol. iii. "These oxen are of the bigness and color of our bulls, but their horns are not so great. They have a great bunch upon their fore-shoulders, and more hair upon their fore part than on their hinder part ; and it is like wool. They have, as it were, a horse mane upon their back bone, and much hair, and very long from the knees downward. They have great tufts of hair hanging down their foreheads, and it seemeth they have beards, because of the great store of hair hanging down at their chins and throats. The males have very long tails, and a great knob or flock at the end, so that in some respects they resemble the lion, and in some other the camel. They push with their horns, they run, they overtake and kill a horse when they are in their rage and anger. Finally, it is a fierce beast of countenance and form of body. The horses fled from them, either be- cause of their deformed shape, or else because they had never seen them. Their mas- ters have no other riches nor substance ; of them they eat, they drink, they apparel, they shoe themselves ; and of their hides they make many things, as houses, shoes, apparel, and ropes; of their bones they make bodkins ; of their sinews and hair, thread ; of their horns, maws and bladders, vessels ; of their dung, fire ; and of their calf skins, budgets, wherein they draw and keep water. To be short, they make so many things of them as they have need of, or as may suffice them in the use of this life."

five days on the journey, and even then much time was lost. The first time it had taken thirty-seven days."*

"On the road they passed a great number of salt marshes where there was a considerable quantity of salt. Pieces longer than tables and four or five inches thick were seen floating on the surface. On the plains they found an immense number of small animals resembling squirrels, and numerous holes burrowed by them in the earth."† These animals were most unquestionably the little prairie-dogs whose villages have been so naively described by Washington Irving and George Wilkins Kendall. On this march the army reached the river Cicuyé, more than thirty leagues below the place where they had before crossed it by a bridge. They then ascended the river, by following the banks, to the town of Cicuyé. The guides declared that this river, the Cicuyé, (no doubt the Pecos,) at a distance of more than twenty days' journey, threw itself into that of Tiguex, (the Rio Grande,) and that subsequently it flowed toward the east. Castañeda goes on to say: "It is believed that it (the Tiguex) joins the great river of Espiritu Sancto (Mississippi River) that the party of Hernando de Soto discovered in Florida."‡

The army under Arellano reaching Tiguex, on its return from the prairies in the month of July, 1541, this officer immediately ordered Captain Francisco de Barrio-Nuevo to ascend the Rio de Tiguex (Rio Grande) in another direction with some soldiers on an exploring expedition. They reached the provinces, one of which, comprising seven villages, was called Hemes; the other, Yuque-Yunque.

Twenty leagues (68 miles) further in ascending the river, they came to a large and powerful village named Braba, to which the Spaniards gave the new title of Valladolid. "It was built on the two banks of the river, which was crossed by bridges built with nicely-squared timber."§ The country was very high and cold. From Braba the exploring party returned to Tiguex. Another party, it seems, went down the Rio de Tiguex (Rio Grande) eighty leagues, where they discovered four large villages, and "reached a place where the river plunged beneath the ground; but inasmuch as their orders confined them to a distance of eighty leagues, they did not push on to the place where, according to the Indians' accounts, this stream escapes again from the earth with considerably augmented volume." ‖

---

* Castañeda's Relations, pp. 133, 134.

† Castañeda's Relations, Ternaux Compans, p. 134.

‡ "VARIOUS NAMES OF THE MISSISSIPPI RIVER.—I remember to have seen in the course of my reading the following Indian, Spanish, and French names applied to the river Mississippi; and it may be well to record them in your magazine for preservation, and probably to be augmented in number by other students of American history:

"*Indian names.*—Mico—king of rivers; Mescha-Sibi-Mescha, great and Sibi River; Namosi-Sipon—Fish River; Okimo-chitto—Great Water path—a Choctá name; Missecsecpo; Meact-chassipi—old father of rivers, according to Du Pratz; Malbouchia, according to Iberville.

"*French.*—Riviere de St. Louis; Riviere de Colbert; Mississippi.

"*Spanish.*—Rio Grande; Rio Grande del Espiritu Santo; Rio de la Eulata; Rio de la Palisada; Rio de Chuchaqua.

"The Vernei Ptolemy of 1513 lays it down, or, at least, marks a river without a name, at the site of its embonchure. Orbus Typis, 1515; Piñeda's map, 1519; other Ptolemies, 1525; Cabeça de Vaca saw it in 1528. De Soto crossed it in June, 1541, and died in Louisiana, on the west bank of the Mississippi, opposite the mouth of the Big Black River, May 21, 1542.

                                    "BRANTZ MAYER.

"BALTIMORE, October 15, 1857."

—(See Historical Magazine, vol. 1, p. 342.)

§ Castañeda's Relations, Ternaux Compans, p. 139.

‖ Castañeda's Relations, Ternaux Compans, p. 140. Mr. Albert Gallatin, commenting on this passage, says: "The assertion that the river was lost under ground was a mistake.

We shall now return to Coronado, whom we left at Quivira. It appears that, in consequence of his not arriving at Tiguex at the expected time, Don Tristan d'Arellano set out in search of him with forty horsemen. At Cicuyé the inhabitants attacked Don Tristan, by which he was delayed four days. Hearing of the approach of Coronado, he contented himself with guarding the passes in the vicinity of the village till the arrival of the general. Castañeda says that, "notwithstanding he had good guides, and was not incumbered with baggage, Coronado was forty days in making the journey from Quivira."* From Cicuyé he journeyed to Tiguex, where he went into winter quarters, with the intention in the spring of pursuing his discoveries by pushing his whole army toward Quivira.

"When winter was over Coronada ordered the preparation to be made for the march to Quivira. Every one then began to make his arrangements. Nevertheless, as often happens in the Indies, things did not turn out as people intended, but as God pleased. One day of festival the general went forth on horseback, as was his custom, to run at the ring with Don Pedro Maldonado. He was mounted on an excellent horse, but his valets having changed the girth of his saddle and having taken a rotten one, it broke in mid-course and the rider unfortunately fell near Don Pedro, whose horse was in full career, and in springing over his body kicked him in the head, thus inflicting an injury which kept him a long while in bed and placed him within two fingers of death."†

The result of this was that being of a superstitious nature and having been foretold by a certain mathematician of Salamanca, who was his friend, that he should one day find himself the omnipotent lord of a distant country, but that he should have a fall which would cause his death, he was very anxious to hasten home to die near his wife and children. From this time, Castañeda states, that Coronado, feigning himself to be more ill than he was, worked upon his soldiery in so subtle a way as to induce the greater part of them to petition him to return to New Spain. They then began openly to declare their belief that it was better to return, inasmuch as no rich country had been found, and it was not populous enough to distribute it among the army. The general, finding no one to oppose him, took up his line of march on his return to

This was, undoubtedly, the place in latitude 31° 39′, where the Rio del Norte, cutting through the mountains, empties into a deep and impassable cañon, from which it emerges some distance below, as has been before stated." (See Transactions of American Ethnological Society, vol. ii, p. 71.)

Mr. Gallatin, though usually very judicious in his remarks, I think is at fault here. The cause of the river disappearing at the point referred to, and then appearing again further down, was not on account of its entering a cañon, which the Spaniards could have noticed and not been deceived about, but because the Rio Tiguex, (Rio Grande,) like most of the rivers which I have seen on the plains and in New Mexico, is liable, when very low, to be lost in its sandy bed, and then to appear again further down, where the sand is not sufficient to absorb it. It is on this account, as I have seen, when the heat of the sun added its potent influence to cause a river to disappear through the day, that during the night, when this influence did not prevail, it would again appear a running stream.

Humboldt refers to a disappearance of the Rio Grande, which appears to have taken place about the same locality, and also attributes it to a wrong cause. "The inhabitants of Paso del Norte preserve the memory of a very extraordinary event which occurred in the year 1752. They saw, all at once, the river become dry, thirty leagues above, and more than twenty leagues below, El Paso; the water of the river precipitated itself in a newly-formed crevasse, and did not appear again above ground until you reach the Presidio de San Elezario." (Humboldt's Essai Politique Sur le Royaume de la Nouvelle Hispagne, edition 1811, p. 303.)

* Castañeda's Relations, Ternaux Compans, p. 142.
† Castañeda's Relations, Ternaux Compans, p. 202.

Mexico in the beginning of April, 1542. He returned by the way of Cibola and Chichilticale, as he had come. At length, after skirmishing with the Indians, in which a number of their men and horses were killed, the army reached Culiacan. From this place Coronado departed for the city of Mexico, to make his report to the viceroy, only about one hundred of his army continuing with him. "Castañeda says he was badly received by the viceroy, who nevertheless gave him a discharge; yet he lost his reputation and soon after his government of New Galicia also."[*]

Thus ended this great expedition, which for extent in distance traveled, duration in time, extending from the spring of 1540 to the summer of 1542, or more than two years, and the multiplicity of its coöperating branch explorations, equaled, if it did not exceed, any land expedition that has been undertaken in modern times.

Having given a general account of the routes pursued by Coronado and his army and of the track of the transport vessels under Alarcon, I will now proceed to fix definitely, so far as I have been enabled, the position of the several important places mentioned by Castañeda and other chroniclers.

The first important point after leaving the city of Mexico is Compostella, where the army rendezvoused preparatory to its setting out on its expedition. This point reached, the army, in an organized condition, took up its line of march along the foot of the west base of the Sierra Nevada in the direction, west of north, as far as Sonora, on the Sonora River; from this place its course was most probably more directly towards Chichilticale, or northerly, through the mountains, as far as the plains of the lower portion of the Rio Santa Cruz, over which it continued its march to Chichilticale.

The towns of Compostella, Culiacan, Cinaloa, and Sonora, points of the routes, are laid down from the "military map of the United States," recently issued from the office of the Chief of Engineers United States War Department. The other points are laid down from data obtained as follows: Chiametla, from "American Atlas, by Mr. Thomas Jeffreys, London, A. D. 1775;" Petatlan, 30 leagues north of Culiacan according to Castañeda,[†] and four days' journey according to Jaramillo.[‡]

With regard to the position of the town of Corazones, it is difficult, on account of the vagueness of the narratives of Jaramillo and Coronado, to fix it. Jaramillo speaks of it as having been situated about five days' journey northwardly from the Yaquemi River, and conveys the idea that it was near or on the Rio Sonora.[§] Castañeda says, " in the lower part of the valley of Sonora is that of the Corazones, inhabited by Spaniards."[||] Again, "Don Tristan decided to found and colonize a town called San Hieronimo de los Corazones; but seeing that it could not prosper in this valley, he transferred it to a place called Senora,

---

[*] Castañeda's Relations, Ternaux Compans, p. 227. Gomora says, "It grieved Don Antonio de Mendoça very much that the army returned home, for he had spent about three-score thousand *pesos* of gold in the enterprise and owed a great part thereof still. Many sought to have dwelt there, but Francisco Vasquez de Coronado, who was rich and lately married a fair wife, would not consent, saying that they could not maintain nor defend themselves in so poor a country and so far from succor. They traveled about 900 leagues in this country." (The rest of the voyage to Acuco, Tiguex, Cicuic, and Quivira, from the General History of the West Indies, by Francis Lopez de Gomora, as quoted by Hakluyt, vol. iii.)

[†] Castañeda's Relations, Ternaux Compans, p. 223.

[‡] Jaramillo's Relations, p. 365.

[§] Jaramillo's Relations, Ternaux Compans, p. 366.

[||] Castañeda's Relations, p. 157.

(Sonora,) and it has been so called to this day."* Again, in another part of his Relations, describing the places between the Sonora River and Chichilticale, he informs us that " it was forty leagues from Sonora to the valley of the Suya, where was founded the city of San Hieronimo."† Now, my idea is, that the town of Corazones on the Sonora River was Sonora, so called because it was eminently the town of the province of Corazones, in which it was situated; and that San Hieronimo de los Corazones was situated, according to Coronado, ten or twelve leagues from the sea,‡ and, as above stated, forty leagues from Sonora, on the Suya River; which would place it about where I have located it, on a river which is now called the San Ignacio.†

From Sonora the march was, according to Jaramillo, four days to the Nexpa River. Jaramillo says: "After leaving Sonora we made a journey of four days in a desert, and arrived at another stream, which we understood was called Nexpa. We descended the stream two days, and we quitted it to the right at a foot of a chain of mountains, which we followed two days. They told us that it was called Chichilticale. After having left the mountains we came to a deep creek, the banks of which were escarped. After quitting this stream, which is beyond the Nexpa of which I have spoken, we took a northeast direction," &c.||

Now the Nexpa, the stream they descended two days, I believe was. the Santa Cruz, running in a northerly direction, (the proper direction of their march;) the mountains, at the foot of which they also traveled two days, were the "Santa Catarina Mountains;" and the stream which they then reached was the Gila, whose deep bed and escarped banks so exactly correspond with the description given by Jaramillo.¶

The next important place was Chichilticale. Here was the Casa Grande of which so much had been reported, and here the army commenced its march northeastwardly across the great desert, on the far side of which were the seven cities of Cibola. That the Casa Grande was so situated, with regard to Cibola, there is no dispute; but of its exact location there is some question.

Castañeda says: " At Chichilticale the country ceases to be covered with thorny trees, and changes its aspect; it is there the gulf terminates, and the coast turns *(O'est la que le golfe se termine et que la côte tourne;)* the mountains follow the same direction, and they must be crossed to reach the plains again."**

---

* Castañeda's Relations, p. 44.   † Ibid., p. 158.
‡ The sea (Gulf of California) returneth towards the west, right against the Corazones, the space of ten or twelve leagues. (Coronado's Rel., Hakluyt, vol. iii, p. 448.)
§ In this connection it may be pertinent to remark, that San Hieronimo de los Corazones, which seems to have been a sort of depôt, was transferred to Sonora; but appears still to have been kept as a post, for we are told that some of its garrison deserted it, for, among other reasons, that they looked on it as useless, "for the road to New Spain passed by a more favorable direction, leaving Suya to the right." This will account for two routes being laid down on the accompanying map between Sonora and the Nexpa River.
|| Jaramillo's Relations, Ternaux Compans, pp. 367 and 368.
¶ Mr. E. G. Squier supposes the Nexpa to have been the Rio Gila. His language is: "Allowing 30 miles to the day's march, which is about the average under favorable circumstances, we have 120 miles as the distance between the point on the Sonora River left by Coronado in his advance and Chichilticale, between longitudes 109° and 110°. This is, according to the best maps, about the distance between the Sonora River and the Gila, called Nexpa by the chronicler." (American Review for November, 1848, p. 6.)
I cannot agree with Mr. Squier in the foregoing statement, for the reason that the distance between the Sonora River and the Gila, according to the latest map issued by the Engineer Department of the Army, is not 120 miles, but as much as 290 miles; and, therefore, as many as eight or ten days' journey instead of four.
** Castañeda's Relations, Ternaux Compans, p. 160.

2

Now this certainly shows that Castañeda believed Chichilticale was situated at the head of the Gulf of California. But according to Coronado's report to the viceroy Mendoça, this assuredly was not the case; for he says: "I departed for the Corazones, and always kept by the sea-coast as near as I could judge, and, in very deed, I still found myself the farther off, in such sort that, when I arrived at Chichilticale, I found myself ten days' journey from the sea, and the father provincial (Marcos de Niça) said that it was only five leagues distant, and he had seen the same. We all conceived great grief, and were not a little confounded, when we saw that we found everything contrary to the information which he had given to your lordship."[*]

In another place, Coronado states that the transport ships which had been ordered to coöperate with him had been seen off the country of the Corazones, on their way to "discover the haven of Chichilticale, which Marcos de Niça said was in five-and-thirty degrees."[†]

The above certainly shows that both De Niça and Castañeda at one time believed that Chichilticale was at the head of the gulf; and it is probable that both the transport vessels and army were ordered to communicate with each other at that point, on the supposition that it was a good harbor, and would be a capital place for a depot of supplies before entering the great desert. But Coronado's report effectually explodes the idea of its having been found such; and if there were more proof on this point needed, it would appear in the fact that neither Alarcon, who commanded the fleet and passed up the Colorado River in search of the army, nor Melchior Diaz, who explored all around the head of the gulf, make any mention of having seen the place, which they most assuredly would have done had they passed anywhere near it.

But where was the exact location of Chichilticale? In my opinion it was on the Rio Gila at Casa Grande, in latitude 33° 4′ 21″ north, and longitude 111° 45′ west from Greenwich, and the following are my reasons therefor:

It is distinctly stated by Castañeda that the place was marked by a Casa Grande, which, though then in ruins on account of having been destroyed by the natives, had evidently been used as a fortress; that it had been built of red earth, and was evidently the work of a civilized people who had come from a distance.[‡]

Now, the first ruin to be seen on the Gila, ascending it from its mouth, and the only one along its whole course which bears any resemblance to that mentioned by Castañeda, and of which we have any record, is that described by Father Font, who, with Father Garces, saw it in 1775,

* Hakluyt's Voyages, vol. iii, p. 448.   †Ibid.

‡ Castañeda's Relations, pp. 40, 101, 162. Mr. Morgan, in a foot-note to his paper before referred to, says: "There is no ruin on the Gila at the present time that answers the above description," and seems to have come to this conclusion, because Captain A. R. Johnston, United States Army, in his journal, (U. S. Ex. Doc. No. 41, 1848, p. 596,) says, "The house was built of a sort of white earth and pebbles, probably containing lime." Emory merely says, "The walls were formed of layers of mud," (Thirtieth Congress, First Session, Ex. Doc. No. 7, p. 82;) and Bartlett in his Personal Narrative, p. 272, informs us that "The walls are laid with large square blocks, and the material is the mud of the valley mixed with gravel."

Mr. N. H. Hutton, civil engineer, assistant to Lieutenant Whipple, in his explorations for the Pacific Railroad in 1853–'54, and at present my assistant, assures me that he has seen the locality and the ruins, and that the Casa had evidently been built of the earth in the vicinity, which is of a reddish color, though in certain reflections of the same the building appeared whitish, on account of the pebbles contained in the mass. Castañeda in his Relations, p. 41, says: "Cette maison, construite en terre rouge;" and p. 161, "La terre de ces pays est rouge." In addition, what more natural than that Emory and Bartlett, finding the color of the building nothing different from that of the soil in that region, should fail to say anything about it?

on their journey to Monterey and the port of San Francisco, and which same ruin was subsequently visited and described by Emory, of the Corps of Topographical Engineers, in 1847.

Father Font's description of it is as follows:

" On the 3d of October, 1775, the commandant ordered us to halt, in order that we might visit the Casa Grande, known by the name of Monte-suma, situated one league from the Rio Gila. We were accompanied by some Indians, and by the governor of Uturituc, who related to us on the way the tradition he had received from his ancestors about this house, some of the particulars of which are doubtless fabulous and others again true.

" The latitude of the locality we found by an observation of the sun to be 33½°.

" The Casa Grande, or palace of Montesuma, must have been built five hundred years previously, (in the thirteenth century,) if we are to believe the accounts given by the Indians; for it appears to have been con-structed by the Mexicans at the epoch of their emigration when the devil, conducting them through different countries, led them to the promised land of Mexico. The house is seventy feet from north to south, and fifty from east to west.* The interior walls are four feet in thick-ness; they are well constructed; the exterior walls are six feet thick. The edifice is constructed of earth, in blocks of different thickness, and has three stories. We found no traces of stairways; we think they must have been burnt when the Apaches burnt this edifice."†

Emory's description, evidently of this same building—for the old maps place Father Font's Casa Grande on the Rio Gila, just above the Pima village, where Emory locates it—is as follows: "About the time of noon halt, a large pile which seemed the work of human hands was seen to the left. It was the remains of a three-story mud-house sixty feet square, pierced for doors and windows. The whole interior of the house had been burnt out, and the walls much defaced."‡

This description, though not precisely the same as that of Father Font, yet is sufficiently close, with the identity of the location, as before stated, to show that they have reference to the same building. Now, Emory by astronomical observation found the latitude of his camp near this locality to be 33° 4' 21" north, and the longitude west from Green-wich 111° 45'. Father Font, as before stated, determined the latitude to be 33½°; but as Emory had, without doubt, far superior instruments, his results are preferable.

We have then, as we think, located Chichilticale, the site of Casa Grande, with a strong probability of accuracy.

On Squier's map of Coronado's route, accompanying the paper on this subject, in the Transactions of the Ethnological Society, (vol. 2,) by Albert Gallatin, I perceive that he makes Coronado to cross the Gila at Casa Grande, but places the latter in about latitude 32°, and longitude 110°; or more than a degree too far south, and nearly two degrees too far to the east. Now, as Juan Jaramillo, who was a captain in Coro-nado's expedition, in his report says the general direction of their march from Chichilticale to Cibola was northeast,§ a line drawn from Chichil-

---

* A Spanish foot is 0.91319 of an English foot. (United States Ordnance Manual.)
† Journal of Father Font, of the college of Santa Cruz of Queretaro. Appendix VII, Casteneda's Relations, Ternaux Compans' Collections; see also Humboldt's "Essai Poli-tique Sur la Royaume de la Nouvelle Espagne," edition of 1811, pp. 36, 297, 298.
‡ Notes of a military reconnoissance made by Lieutenant Colonel William H. Emory, Corps of Topographical Engineers, in 1846–'47, with the advance guard of the Army of the West, p. 82.
§ Juan Jaramillo's Relations, Ternaux Compans' Collections, pp. 368, 369.

ticale as laid down on Squier's map would not pass through or near Zuñi, (identical on his map with Cibola,) as it ought to do, but more than a degree to the east of it; thus showing his position of Chichilticale manifestly erroneous.

Again, on the map of R. H. Kern, accompanying "Schoolcraft's History of the Indian Tribes of North America," he places Chichilticale as much as a degree of latitude south of the Gila and in longitude 109°. Here again a line in a northeast direction from Chichilticale would not pass, as it should, through or near Zuñi, (identical, as Kern thinks, with Cibola,) but more than two degrees to the eastward of it; which also shows his position of Chichilticale very considerably out of the way.

The next and most important inquiry is the exact locality of the seven cities of Cibola. Gallatin, Squier, Whipple, Professor Turner, and Kern, have contended for Zuñi and its vicinity. Emory and Abert, on the contrary, have conjectured that Cibolletta, Moquino, Pojnati, Covero, Acoma, Laguna, and Poblacon, a group of villages some ninety miles to the eastward of Zuñi, furnish the site of the seven cities; and Mr. Morgan, as I have before remarked, in the North American Review for April, 1869, has advanced the idea that the ruins on the Chaco, lying about one hundred miles to the northeast of Zuñi, more completely satisfy all the conditions of the problem which the accounts of Coronado's journey, by Castañeda and others, have imposed on its solution. To my mind, however, Zuñi and vicinity present the strongest claims to being considered the site of the renowned cities, and the following are my reasons therefor:

It seems that from Chichilticale to Cibola, the direction of Coronado's route, according to Jaramillo, as before remarked, was generally northeast; and from Coronado's report I extract in relation to it as follows. He is speaking of what occurred after leaving Chichilticale:

"I entered the confines of the desert, on Saint John's day eve, and to refresh our former travels we found no grass, but worser way of mountains and bad passages where we had passed already; and the horses being tired were greatly molested therewith; but after we had passed these thirty leagues, we found fresh rivers and grasses like that of Castile, &c.; and there was flax, but chiefly near the banks of a certain river, which, therefore, was called El Rio del Lino, that is to say, the River of Flax; we found no Indians at all for a day's travel, but afterward four Indians came out unto us in peaceable manner, saying that they were sent over to that desert place to signify unto us that we were welcome."[*]

In addition to the foregoing, Castañeda says that in about fifteen days from Chichilticale "they arrived within eight leagues of Cibola, upon the banks of a river they called the Vermejo, on account of its red color;"[†] and Jaramillo remarks that in approaching Cibola "always in the same direction, that is to say, toward the northeast, they came to a river which they called the Vermejo; that here they met one or two Indians, who afterwards they recognized as belonging to the first village of Cibola; and that they reached this village in two days from when they had first met them."[‡]

Now let any one consult the accompanying map, reduced from the latest map issued by the Engineer Bureau at Washington, and he will

---

* Hakluyt's Voyages, vol. iii, p. 449.
† Castañeda's Relations, Ternaux Compans, p. 41.
‡ Jaramillo's Relations, Ternaux Compans, p. 369.

see that Coronado's march from Chichilticale, or Casa Grande, must have been very nearly coincident with the route there laid down, to wit: in a *northeasterly* direction for the first thirty leagues, over the rough Pinal and Mogollon Mountains; and then getting on the tributaries of the *Rio del Lino*, or Flax River, where he found "fresh water and grasses," he followed up the Vermejo, or Colorado River, to Cibola, or Zuñi of the present day and its vicinity, where he found the other six cities. The distance by such route, between Chichilticale and Zuñi, would be about 270 miles, or require a journey of 17 days, (about 16 miles a day,) the time it took Coronado to accomplish the distance;* and this agrees quite exactly with the distance, 80 leagues, as given by Castañeda in another place.†

But there are other good reasons for this belief. At Zuñi and its vicinity, within a distance of about 16 miles, and on the banks of the Vermejo, or Little Colorado River, there are the ruins of as many as six pueblos, all showing that they were once built of stone; and, with the present Zuñi, doubtless they constituted the "seven cities" which, according to Coronado, were all built "within four leagues together,"‡ and according to Castañeda were "situated in a very narrow valley between *des Montagnes Escarpées*,"§ which may have been intended to mean escarped *mesas*, or table lands, just as close in the valley of the Little Colorado or Rio de Zuñi.

In my report to the Chief of Topographical Engineers of my reconnoissance made in the Navajo country in 1848, I described Zuñi as follows: "The pueblo of Zuñi, when first seen about three miles off, appeared like a low ridge of brownish rocks, not a tree being visible to relieve the nakedness of its appearance. It is a pueblo or Indian town, situated on the Rio de Zuñi. This river at the town has a bed of about 150 yards wide. The stream, however, at the time we saw it, only showed a breadth of about 6 feet and a depth of a few inches. It is represented as running into the Colorado of the West. The town, like Santo Domingo, is built terrace-shaped, each story—of which there are generally three—as you ascend being smaller laterally, so that one story answers, in fact, for the platform of the one above it. It, however, is far more compact than Santo Domingo, its streets being narrow, and in places presenting the appearance of tunnels or covered ways, on account of the houses extending at these places over them."‖

Lieutenant A. W. Whipple, Corps Topographical Engineers, visited the ruins of old Zuñi in 1853–'54, and in his report to the War Department thus describes the place: "We took a trail and proceeded two miles south to a deep cañon, where were springs of water. Thence by a zigzag course we led our mules up the first bench of ascent. At various points of the ascent, where a projecting rock permitted, were barricades of stone walls, from which, the old man (his guide) told us, they had hurled rocks upon the invading Spaniards. Having ascended, according to our estimate, 1,000 feet, we found ourselves upon a level surface covered with thick cedars. The top of the *mesa* was of an irregular figure a mile in width, and bounded on all sides by perpendicular cliffs. Three times we crossed it, searching in vain for the trace of a

---

* Castaneda's Relations, pp. 41, 42.
† Ibid., p. 188.
‡ Coronado's Relations, Hakluyt, vol. iii, p. 451.
§ Castañeda's Relations, Ternaux Compans, p. 164.
‖ "Journal of a military reconnoissance from Santa Fé, New Mexico, to the Navajo country, made by Lieutenant J. H. Simpson, Corps of Topographical Engineers, in 1849," United States Senate Ex. Doc. No. 64, 31st Congress, 1st session, 1850; also, Lippincott, Grambo & Co., Philadelphia, 1852, pp. 89 and 90.

ruin. But the guide hurried us on half a mile further, when appeared the ruins of a city indeed. Crumbling walls from 2 to 12 feet high were crowded together in confused heaps over several acres of ground. Upon examining the pueblo we found that the standing walls rested upon ruins of greater antiquity. The primitive masonry, as well as we could judge, must have been about 6 feet thick. The more recent was not more than a foot, but the small sandstone blocks had been laid in mud mortar with considerable care."*

Now I take it that old Zuñi was one of the seven towns of Cibola, called by Coronado "Grenada, because it was somewhat like to it;"† and the *narrow winding way*, ascending which Coronado was knocked down by stones hurled upon him by the defenders,‡ was in all probability the very zigzag approach mentioned by Whipple, and which he found so difficult in his ascent to the ruins.

The other six towns were doubtless Zuñi of the present day, and those whose ruins are to be found still further up the valley, showing they had been stone structures, and to which I refer in my report before referred to, as follows: "Within a few yards of us are several heaps of pueblo ruins. Two of them, on examination, I found to be of elliptical shape and approximating 1,000 feet in circuit. The buildings seem to have been chiefly built on the periphery of an ellipse, having a large interior court; but their style and the details of their construction, except that they were built of stone and mud mortar, are not distinguishable in the general mass. The areas of each are now so overgrown with bushes and so much commingled with mother earth as, except on critical examination, to be scarcely distinguishable from natural mounds. The usual quantum of pottery lies scattered around. The governor of Zuñi, who is again on a visit to us, informs us that the ruins I have just described, as also those seen a couple of miles back, are the ruins of pueblos which his people formerly inhabited."§

There are other circumstances of relative position of places which point most indubitably to the same conclusion; as follows: Castañeda repeatedly states that Cibola was the *first* inhabited province they met going north from Chichilticale *after* they crossed the desert, and the *last* they left *before entering* the desert on their return to Mexico. Again, the present relations to each other of Zuñi and the Moqui Pueblos, and also of Acoma, perched on a mesa height, in regard to courses and distances tally sufficiently near with the positions of Tusayan and Acuco, as given by Castañeda, namely, the former northwest 25 leagues and the latter eastwardly five days' journey from Cibola,‖ as to make it exceedingly probable that they refer to the same localities.¶ Again, Castañedo,

---

* Pacific R. R. Reports, vol. iii, pp. 68, 69.
† Coronado's Relation, Hakluyt, vol. iii, p. 451.
‡ "Cependant il fallait s'emparer de Cibola ce qui n'était pas chose facile, car le chemin qui y conduissat était étroit et tortueux. Le Général fut renversé d'un coup de pierre en montant à l'assaut," &c. Castañeda's Rel., Ternaux Compans, p. 43.
§ Simpson's Journal, p. 97.
‖ Castañeda's Relations, Ternaux Compans, pp. 58, 67, 68, 69, 70, 165.
¶ Mr. Squier, in his article on the "Ancient Monuments, &c., in New Mexico and California," in American Review for November, 1848, gives the position of Tusayan from Cibola, *both* northeast and northwest from Cibola, and on his map accompanying Mr. Albert Gallatin's Essay, in the Transactions of the American Ethnological Society, vol. ii, he has placed it in a northeast direction. The proper direction of Tusayan with regard to Cibola is northwest. (See Castañeda's Relations, Ternaux Compans, p. 165.) Besides Cardenas, on his way to the Rio del Tizon, (Colorado,) passed through Tusayan from Cibola, which makes it all very natural if Tusayan was northwest from Cibola, but would not be so if it was in a northeast direction, as laid down on Mr. Squier's map.

describing the valley in which the province of Cibola was situated, says, " Cest une vallée trés-etroite entre des montagnes escarpées,"* which is an exact description of the valley of the Rio de Zuñi, confined between the walls of inclosing mesas. Again, Jaramillo says " this first village of Cibola is exposed a little towards the northeast, and to the northwest in about five days' journey is a province of seven villages called Tusayan,† all of which exactly accords with the exposed position to the northeast of old Zuñi and correctly describes the location of the Moqui villages.

But there is some historical evidence upon this point which I consider irrefragable, and which certainly makes Zuñi and Cibola identical places.

Referring to the relation of a notable journey made by Antonio de Espejo to New Mexico, in 1583, to be found in Hakluyt's Voyages, vol. iii, I read as follows: "Antonio de Espejo also visited Acoma, situated upon a high rock which was about 50 paces high, having no other entrance but by a ladder or pair of stairs hewn into the same rock, whereat our people marveled not a little.

" Twenty-five leagues from hence, toward the west, they came to a certain province called by the inhabitants themselves Zuñi, and by the Spaniards Cibola, containing a great number of Indians, in which province .Francisco Vasquez de Coronado had been, and had erected many crosses and other tokens of Christianity, which remained as yet standing. Here also they found three Indian Christians who had remained there ever since the said journey, whose names were Andrew de Culiacan, Gaspar de Mexico, and Antonio de Guadalajara, who had about forgotten their language, but could speak the country speech very well; howbeit after some small conference with our men they easily understood one another."

Now turning to Castaneda's Relations, where he gives an account of Coronado's leaving the country for Mexico, I find his language as follows : " When the army arrived at Cibola it rested for a while to prepare itself for entering the desert, for it is the last point inhabited. We left the country entirely peaceful ; there were some Indians from Mexico who had accompanied us,, who remained there and established themselves, (il y ent même quelques Indiens du Mexique qui nous avaient accompagnés, qui y restèrent et s'y établirent.")‡

Thus it would seem that the two accounts of Espejo and Castañeda correspond in such a manner as not to leave the slightest doubt that Zuñi of the present day is the Cibola of old. Coronado left three of his men at Cibola, who were found living there by Espejo and his party forty years afterwards ; they had nearly forgotten their original language, but yet, after awhile, managed to converse with some of Espejo's men. What more natural, and, indeed, what could have been a more interesting topic than the adventures of these men ; how they got there, and whether Zuñi was veritably the far-famed Cibola that forty years previously had excited the attention of the governments of New and Old Spain. Espejo, under the above circumstances, reporting that the Spaniards called Zuñi Cibola, certainly could not have meant anything else than that he believed it veritably such. I have been thus particular with regard to this testimony, for the reason that Mr. Morgan, in his essay already referred to, while he recognizes the historical fact of Zuñi having been called by the Spaniards, according to Espejo's Relations, Cibola, in 1583, yet advances the idea that after all Espejo probably

* Castañeda's Relations, Ternaux Compans, p. 164.
† Jaramillo's Relations, Ternaux Compans, p. 370.
‡ Castañeda's Relations, Ternaux Compans, p. 217.

only meant to express that they conjectured the places to have been identical.

It seems to me that what I have advanced shows most conclusively that Cibola and Zuñi are identical localities, and nothing could be said which could make it more certain; but as corroborative I will state that I have seen in the excellent library of the Peabody Institute of Baltimore an atlas entitled "The American Atlas, or a Geographical Description of the whole Continent of America, by Mr. Thomas Jeffreys, Geographer, published in London in 1773." On map No. 5 of this atlas, Zuñi and Cibola are laid down as synonymous names, and the locality they express is precisely that of Zuñi of the present day.* Again, on a "Carte contenant le Royaume du Mexique et La Floride," in the "Atlas Historique par Mr. C * * * avec des dissertations sur l'Histoire de chaque etat par Mr. Guendeville," tome vi, second edition, published in Amsterdam, 1732, I find Zuñi and Cibola laid down as synonymous.

In this connection it may be proper to observe that the claims of Ciboletta, Moquino, Poquate, Covero, Acomo, Laguna, Poblacon, as conjectured by Emory and Abert to be regarded as the seven cities of Cibola, are rendered null by the historical fact mentioned by Castañeda, and also by Jaramillo, that the latter were situated on the Rio Vermejo, (Little Colorado,) a tributary of the Southern Ocean;† and also by the circumstance of the army, on its march from Cibola to Tiguex, finding Acuco (Acoma) five days' journey to the eastward of Cibola, a circumstance which could not have taken place if Acuco (Acoma) were one of the seven towns of Cibola. Besides, Castañeda, in enumerating the villages dispersed in the country, expressly states that "Cibola is the first province; it contains seven villages; Tusayan, seven; the rock of Acuco, one, &c.,‡ which certainly shows that Cibola and Acuco were separate and district provinces.

Again, I cannot see that the ruins of the Chaco, which, according to my explorations and reading are probably, on account of their extent and character, the most remarkable yet discovered in this country, have any just claims, as advanced by Mr. Morgan, to be regarded as the seven cities of Cibola;§ first, for the reason that they are not, as required by historical fact, situated on the Rio Vermejo, (Little Colorado,) or tributary of the Rio del Lino or Flax River; second, they are not so situated with regard to the desert passed over by Coronado, between Chichilticale and Cibola, as to make the statement of Castañeda pertinent, to wit,

---

* On this atlas is indorsed, "Presented to the Peabody Institute by the Hon. John P. Kennedy, April 1, 1864. By this map the great dispute between Daniel Webster and Lord Ashburton (relating doubtless to the northeastern boundary) was settled, particularly by map No. 5."

† "All the streams we met, whether rivulet or river, as far as that of Cibola, and I believe even one or two days' journey beyond that place, flow in the direction of the South Sea, (Mer du Sud,) meaning the Pacific Ocean;" further on they flow to the North Sea, (Mer du Nord,) meaning the Gulf of Mexico. Jaramillo's Relations, Ternaux Compans, p. 370.

‡ Castañeda's Relations, Ternaux Compans, pp. 181, 182.

§ Mr. Morgan, in his essay before referred to, having already made large extracts from my report to the Government on these ruins, I deem it unnecessary to say anything further in relation to them than to refer the reader for a more detailed account to said report. It is interesting, however, in this connection, to present the following extract from Humboldt's Essai sur le Royaume de la Nouvelle Espagne, page 305, which in all probability refers to these very ruins: "The Indian traditions inform us that some twenty leagues to the north of Moqui, near the embouchure of the river Zejuannes, a river of the Navajos, was the first resting place (demeure) of the Aztecs after their sortie from Atzlan." Again, on his map accompanying his Essay, is the following: "Première demeure des Aztèques sortés d'Atzlan en 1160, tradition in certaine," in longitude about 112°30″, latitude 37°.

that Cibola was the first village to be met after passing the desert, and the last on leaving the peopled country to enter the desert; third, the Moqui villages (undoubtedly Tusayan) do not lie to the northwest from the ruins on the Chaco, as they should do if these ruins were Cibola, but to the south of west; and fourth, the route of Coronado's army eastward from there to Cicuyé, by the way of Acuco, (Acoma,) would have been very much and unnecessarily out of the proper direction.

Mr. Morgan mentions the fact stated by Coronado, that it was eight days' journey from Cibola to the buffalo range. This, he thinks, could very well have taken place on the hypothesis of the Chaco ruins having been Cibola, but not on the supposition of Zuñi. But the distance of Zuñi to the buffalo range east of the Rio Pecos is only about 230 miles, which certainly could have been reached in eight days, allowing the journey he does of 30 miles per day.

But to proceed with the principal points of Coronado's route eastward from Cibola. I believe that all authorities who have written on the subject concur in the view that the Pueblo of Acoma, or Hak-koo-kee-ah, as it is now called in the Zuñi language, is the Acuco of Colorado. *

The singular coincidence of the names, as well as the striking resemblance of the two places as described by Castañeda and Abert, which cannot be predicated of any other place in New Mexico, together with the proper relation of Acoma to Zuñi (Cibola) and Tiguex in distance and direction, all show that they are identical. †

Bancroft Library

The next province Coronado entered was that of Tiguex. Mr. Gallatin has located it on the Rio Puerco. His language relating to it is as follows: "Having compared those several accounts (of Castañeda and Jaramillo) with Lieutenant Abert's map and with that of Mr. Gregg, it

---

* Lieutenant Colonel J. H. Eaton, United States Army, writing on this subject, remarks: "In a conversation with a very intelligent Zuñi Indian I learned that the Pueblo of Acoma is called in the Zuñi tongue Hak-koo-kee-ah, (Acuco,) and this name was given to me without any previous question which would serve to give him an idea of this old Spanish name. Does not this, therefore, seem to give color to the hypothesis that Coronado's army passed by or near to the present Pueblo of Zuñi, and that it was their Cibola, or one of the seven cities of Cibola." (Schoolcraft's History of the Indian Tribes of the United States, part iv, p. 220.)

† The following graphic description of Acoma is from Abert: "After a journey of 15 miles we arrived at Acoma. High on a lofty rock of sandstone, such as I have described, sits the city of Acoma. On the northern side of the rock the rude boreal blasts have heaped up the sand so as to form a practical ascent for some distance; the rest of the way is through solid rock. At one place a singular opening or narrow way is formed between a huge, square tower of rock and the perpendicular face of the cliff. Then the road winds round like a spiral stairway; and the Indians have, in some way, fixed logs of wood in the rock, radiating from a vertical axis, like steps. These afford foothold to man and beast in clambering up.

"We were constantly meeting and passing Indians, who had their 'burros' laden with peaches. At last we reached the top of the rock, which was nearly level, and contains about sixty acres. Here we saw a large church, and several continuous blocks of buildings, containing sixty or seventy houses in each block. (The wall at the side that faced outward was unbroken, and had no windows until near the top. The houses were three stories high.) In front, each story retreated back as it ascended, so as to leave a platform along the whole front of the story. These platforms are guarded by parapet walls about three feet high. In order to gain admittance you ascend to the second story by means of ladders. The next story is gained by the same means; but to reach the 'azotia,' or roof, the partition walls on the platform that separates the quarters of different families have been formed into steps. This makes quite a narrow staircase, as the walls are not more than one foot in width." (Report of Lieutenant J. W. Abert, Corps Topographical Engineers, of his examination of New Mexico in the years 1846–'47, Ex. Doc. 41, 30th Congress, 1st session, pp. 470, 471.)

appears to me probable that the Tiguex country lay, not on the main Rio Norte, but on its tributary, the Rio Puerco and its branches, and that the river which the Spaniards called Cicuyé, and on which they were obliged to build a bridge, was the main Rio del Norte."*

Mr. W. H. Davis, author of "El Gringo; or New Mexico and her People," published in 1853, takes the same view.

Mr. Squier believes the Rio de Tiguex to have been the Rio Grande, and the Rio de Cicuyé the Pecos, but locates Tiguex on the Rio Grande, *above* the mouth of the Puerco. Messrs. Kern and Morgan take the same view.

According to my investigations I believe the Rio Tiguex to have been the Rio Grande, and the Rio de Cicuyé the Rio Pecos; but while I am willing to admit there are some grounds for the hypothesis that Tiguex was located on the Rio Grande *above* the mouth of the Puerco, yet I think there are still stronger grounds for the belief that it was situated on the Rio Grande *below* that river.

Castañeda says, "Three days' journey from Acuco (Acoma) Alvarado and his army arrived in a province which was called Tiguex."†

Again, "The province of Tignex contains twelve villages, situated on the banks of a great river in a valley about two leagues broad. It is bounded on the west by some mountains, which are very high and covered with snow. Four villages are built at the foot of these mountains and three others upon the heights."‡

Now, as Coronado and his army marched eastward § from Acuco, (Acoma,) and they accomplished the distance in a three days' journey and then came to a large river, on the banks of which was situated the province of Tiguex, it is clear that as the Rio Grande is the first large river to be met eastward from Acuco (Acoma) at a distance varying from sixty to eighty miles, depending on the route taken, this was the great river referred to, or the Rio de Tiguex.

The idea of Mr. Gallatin and Mr. Davis that the Puerco was this river is, I think, entirely untenable, for the reason that this river in its best stage is only about one hundred and twenty miles long, and frequently, as I myself have observed, so dry that its existence could only be inferred from its dry bed and the occasional pools of water to be met along its track. It certainly, then, could not with any propriety be called a *great* river, as the Rio de Tiguex was represented to be.

In addition, we learn that the guides who conducted the army back to Cicuyé, on its return from its search after Quivira, declared that the Rio de Cicuyé threw itself into the Rio de Tiguex more than twenty days' journey (or over four hundred miles) below where they struck it;"‖ which would have been an absurdity if the Tiguex were the trifling Rio Puerco, and the Cicuyé the Rio Grande, as Mr. Gallatin supposed; but which is all very plain on the hypothesis that the Tiguex was the Rio Grande, and the Cicuyé the Pecos.

But where was the exact location of the province of Tiguex?

It was certainly *below* Hemez and Quirix, (San Felipe,¶) for the chron-

* Transactions American Ethnological Society, vol. 2, p. 73.
† Castañeda's Relations, Ternaux Compans, p. 71.
‡ Castañeda's Relations, Ternaux Compans, pp. 167, 168.
§ Ibid, p. 67.
‖ Castañeda's Relations, Ternaux Compans, p. 135.
¶ On the old maps, as also on Humboldt's, illustrating his "Nouvelle Hispagne," I notice the pueblo of San Felipe is laid down as "S. Felipe *de Cueres*," which I am informed is its name at this day. Indeed, Gregg, speaking of certain pueblos in New Mexico, says, "those of Cochiti, Santo Domingo, San Felipe, and perhaps Sandia, speak the same tongue, though they seem formerly to have been distinguished as Queres" (Commerce of the Prairies, 2d edition, vol. i, p. 269.)

icler states that farther to the north (from Tiguex) is the province of Quirix, which contains seven villages; seven leagues to the northwest (which may mean from Quirix or Tiguex) that of Hemez, which contains the same number, &c.;* the text says, "nord-est," but this is evidently a mistake, as the oldest maps extant place Hemez where it is now situated, on the Rio de Hemez, to the west of the Rio Grande.

The foregoing would seem to show conclusively that Tiguex was situated below Quirix, and possibly, under one of the constructions given above, only seven leagues or twenty-four miles below Hemez, which would place it on the Rio Grande just about the mouth of the Rio de Hemez, or about 80 miles above the mouth of the Puerco, where the authorities above given have placed it. But yet the extract before given from Castañeda expressly states also that the "Province of Tiguex was situated upon the banks of a great river (Rio de Tiguex) in a valley about two leagues broad, and bounded on its west by some very high, snowy mountains," &c. Now, the only locality which will answer this description is that part of the valley of the Rio Grande bounded on its west by the Socorro Mountains, situated just below the mouth of the Puerco. These are the first mountains to be met in descending the river from Santo Domingo, or from even above that pueblo, (all the intervening heights being merely table-lands and therefore not so elevated as to be termed snowy,) and they fix the locality, in my judgment, as I have before stated, *below* the mouth of the Puerco.

I have, therefore, on my map located the province of Tiguex on the Rio Grande below the Rio Puerco, at the foot of the Socorro Mountains, which bounds it on its west; and it is somewhat confirmatory of this position that on the map No. 5 of "Thomas Jeffreys' Atlas," before referred to as excellent authority, I find *Tigua*, no doubt intended for the same place, or province, located in the valley of the Rio Grande, just where I have located Tiguex, namely, at the foot of the Socorro Mountains.

The next important place in the route of Coronado from Tiguex was Cicuyé. Castañedo says: "After a journey of five days from Tiguex, Alvarado (with his detachment of twenty men) arrived at Cicuyé, a very well fortified village, the houses of which are four stories high."† Again, "The army quitted Tiguex on the 5th of May (1531) and took the route to Cicuyé, which is twenty-five leagues distant."‡ Jaramillo states the direction to have been "northeast."§ In another place Castañeda remarks that "Cicuyé is built in a narrow valley, in the midst of mountains covered with pines. It is traversed by a small stream, in which we caught some excellent trout."||

Now, all this points, as I believe, to the ruins of Pecos, on the Rio Pecos, as the site of Cicuyé, and in this I agree with Mr. Squier and Mr. Kern. These ruins are in a northeast direction from the supposed position of Tiguex, and about five days' journey distant. They are also situated in a narrow valley in the midst of mountains covered with pines, and the site is traversed by a small silvery stream, in which may be caught some excellent trout. I certainly know no other place that in so many respects suits the conditions of the problem; but the

---

* Castañeda's Relations, Ternaux Compans.
† Castañeda's Relations, Ternaux Compans, p. 71.
‡ Castaneda's Relations, Ternaux Compans, p. 113.
§ Jaramillo's Relations, Ternaux Compans, p. 371.
|| Castañeda's Relations, Ternaux Compans, p. 179.

following remark by Castañeda has perplexed investigators not a little. He remarks, that "when the army quitted Cicuyé to go to Quivira we entered the mountains, which it was necessary to cross to reach the plains, and on the fourth day we arrived at a great river, very deep, which passes also near Cicuyé. It is for this reason we call it the Rio de Cicuyé. Here we were obliged to build a bridge, which employed us four days."*

The difficulty has been to reconcile the statement that Cicuyé (Pecos) was on or near the Rio Cicuyé, and yet that after four days' travel, after traversing some mountains in a northeasterly direction, the army should again cross it by a bridge.

Now all this, I think, can be reconciled by reference to the accompanying map, on which will be found laid down a route, the only one, I believe, existing at the present day between Pecos and Las Végas, on the Rio Gallinas, a tributary of the Rio Pecos, where the plains commence.† The general direction of the road is northeast. It traverses some very rough mountains, and the distance between the two places is about fifty miles, which might have necessitated, considering the roughness of the route, a journey of four days, as the conditions require. Besides, the Gallinas is liable to be flooded from the melting snows of the neighboring sierras in the month of May and fore-part of June; this naturally would make necessary at such times a bridge to cross it. Emory, speaking about Las Végas and its vicinity, says: "As we emerged from the hills into the valley of the Végas, our eyes were greeted for the first time with waving corn. The stream (the Gallinas) was *flooded*, and the little drains by which the fields were irrigated full to the brim."‡

My idea is, then, that this stream being a tributary of the Pecos and larger than the latter at Cicuyé, (Pecos,) it was, in all probability, called for those reasons the Rio de Cicuyé, though the place by this name was situated distant from it on another branch of the same river, where the ruins of the Pecos village are now to be seen.

I will also state, as strongly confirmatory of this location of Cicuyé, that on map No. 5 of the "American Atlas, by Thomas Jeffreys, published in 1775," twice before referred to, I find laid down, in about the present locality of Pecos, a place named "Sayaqué," which might well answer for Cicuyé.

But where was Quivira? "the last" (place,) as Castañeda remarks, "which was visited by Coronado." Mr. Squier, on his map, before referred to, has the route pursued by Coronado laid down as extending indefinitely in a northeastwardly direction, from Cicuyé (Pecos;) but still, in his essay before referred to, says "there is no doubt that Vasquez Coronado penetrated, in 1541, to the region of Gran Quivira, visited and described by Gregg;"§ that is the Quivira which on modern maps is laid down in latitude about 34° north, and longitude 106° west from Greenwich, or about 100 miles directly south from Santa Fé. Lieutenant Abert and Mr. Kern have expressed the same thing; the latter locating Coronado's route, not in a *northeast* direction from Cicuyé and extending about *six hundred* miles, as required by the statements of Castañeda, Coronado, and Jaramillo; but in a direction *almost directly the reverse*—at first eastwardly and then westwardly, so as to make him reach a place called Quivira in modern times, but located only about

---

* Castañeda's Relations, Ternaux Compans, pp. 115, 116.
† This is the only route which for years has been taken by travelers and others from Fort Leavenworth to Santa Fé.
‡ Emory's Report, Ex. Doc. No. 7, 30th Congress, 1st session, p. 26.
§ American Review for November, 1848, p. 6.

one hundred miles from Cicuyó (Pecos,) and that almost in a *due south* direction.

Mr. Gallatin says, "Coronado appears to have proceeded as far north as near the 40° of latitude,"* in search of Quivira.

Again, quoting from him, "Quivira, (referring to that about one hundred miles south from Santa Fé, in latitude 34° and longitude 106°,) about fourteen miles east of Abo, was not visited by Lieutenant Abert; but its position was correctly ascertained. It is quite probable that the place now known by that name was the true Quivira of the Indians at the time of Coronado's expedition. But whether deceived by a treacherous Indian guide, as they assert, or having not understood what the Indians meant, which is quite probable, the Spaniards gave the name of Quivira to an imaginary country situated north and represented as abounding in gold."†

Now, it is something singular that, so far as I have been able to investigate, there is no such place as Quivira laid down on the old maps in the locality where modern maps show it—namely, in latitude 34°, longitude 106°; but there is a place of that name laid down on these maps in about latitude 40°, as high as Coronado located it. I am therefore inclined to believe that at the time of Coronado's expedition the former Quivira did not exist. At all events, it is scarcely credible that such a remarkable city as Quivira was represented to be, so full of gold, &c., situated as it was, *only about fifty miles from Tiguex*, the headquarters of Coronado's army, and which might have been reached in two days, could have been kept from the knowledge and observation of the army for about a year and a half, during all the time that a portion of it was stationed at that place.

Again, Gregg, (an excellent authority,) speaking of the ruins of Quivira, remarks: "By some persons these ruins have been supposed to be the remains of an ancient pueblo, or aboriginal city. That is not probable, however, for though the relics of aboriginal temples might possibly be mistaken for those of Catholic churches, yet it is not to be presumed that the Spanish coat of arms would be found sculptured and painted on their façades, as is the case in more than one instance."‡

No; I am of opinion that Coronado and his army marched just as Castañeda, Jaramillo, and Coronado have reported; that is, generally in a northeast direction, over extensive plains, through countless herds of buffaloes and prairie-dog villages, and at length, after getting in a manner lost, and finding, as the chronicler says, they had gone "too far toward Florida,"§ that is,.to the eastward, and had traveled from Tiguex for thirty-seven days, or a distance of between 700 and 800 miles, their provisions failing them, the main body turned back to Tiguex; and Coronado, with thirty-six picked men, continued his explorations northwardly to the 40° of latitude, where he reached a province which the Indians called Quivira, in which he expected to find a city containing remarkable houses and stores of gold, but which turned out to be only the abode of very wild Indians, who lived in miserable wigwams, and knew nothing about gold.

---

* Transactions American Ethnological Society, vol. ii, p. 64.
† Ibid., p. 95.
‡ Gregg's Commerce of the Prairies, 2d ed., p. 165.
§ On some of the old maps Florida embraces all the country west of the Rio Grande and south of Canada. See "Atlas Historique, par Mr. C * * * ; Avec des dissertations sur l'Histoire de Chaque état, par Mr. Gueudeville," before alluded to, published in 1732. Again, Hakluyt remarks: "The name of Florida was at one time applied to all that tract of territory which extends from Canada to the Rio del Norte." (See his introduction to "The Discovery and Conquest of Peru by Don Fernando de Soto," p. 10.)

Coronado's description of the region is as follows: "The province of Quivira is 950 leagues (3,230 miles) from Mexico. The place I have reached is the 40° of latitude. The earth is the best possible for all kinds of productions of Spain, for while it is very strong and black, it is very well watered by brooks, springs, and rivers. I found prunes like those of Spain, some of which were black, also some excellent grapes and mulberries." *

Jaramillo, who accompanied Coronado to Quivira, speaking of this region, says: "This country (Quivira) has a superb appearance, and such that I have not seen better in all of Spain, neither in Italy nor France, nor in any other country where I have been in the service of your Majesty. It is not a country of mountains; there are only some hills, some plains, and some streams of very fine water, (des ruis-seaux de fort belle eau.) It satisfied me completely. I presume that it is very fertile and favorable for the cultivation of all kinds of fruits."†

In another portion of his Relations he mentions having crossed a large river, to which they gave the name of "Saint Peter and Saint Paul," which very probably was the Arkansas, and after traveling several days farther north, they came to the province of Quivira, where they learned that there was a still larger river farther on, to which they gave the name of "Teucarea," and which I believe to have been the Missouri.‡

Again, Castañeda says: "It is in this country (that of Quivira) that the Espiritu Sancto, (Mississippi,) which Don Fernando de Soto discovered in Florida, takes its source. * * * * The course of this river is so long, and it receives so many affluents, that it is of prodigious length to where it debouches into the sea, and its fresh waters extend far out after you have lost sight of the land."§

All the authors who have written on this subject seem to have discredited Coronado's report that he explored northwardly as far as the 40° of north latitude; but not only do the reports of Castañeda and Jaramillo bear him out in his statement, but the peculiar description of the country as given by them all—namely, that it was *exceedingly rich ;* its soil *black ;* that it bore, spontaneously, grapes and prunes, (wild plums;) was watered by many streams of pure water, &c.; and the circumstance of this kind of country not being found anywhere in the probable direction of Coronado's route, except across the Arkansas and on the headwaters of the Arkansas River; all this, together with the allusion to a large river, the "Saint Peter and Saint Paul," (probably the Arkansas,) which they crossed before reaching Quivira, in lati-

---

* Following the orders of your Majesty (Don Antonio de Mendoça,) I have observed the best possible treatment toward the natives of this province, and of all others that I have traversed. They have nothing to complain of me or my people. I sojourned twenty-five days in the province of Quivira, as much to thoroughly explore the country as to see if I could not find some further occasion to serve your Majesty, for the guides whom I brought with me have spoken of provinces situated still farther on. That which I have been able to learn is, that in all this country one can find neither gold nor any other metal. They spoke to me of small villages, whose inhabitants for the most part do not cultivate the soil. They have huts of hides and of willows, and change their places of abode with the *vaches* (buffaloes.) The tale they told me then (that Quivira was a city of extraordinary buildings and full of gold) was false. In inducing me to part with all my army to come to this country, the Indians thought that the country being desert and without water, they would conduct us into places where our horses and ourselves would die of hunger; that is what the guides have confessed. They told that they had acted by the advice of the natives of these countries. (Coronado's Relations, Ternaux Compans, pp. 360, 361.)

† Jaramillo's Relations, Ternaux Compans, p. 378.

‡ Jaramillo's Relations, Ternaux Compans, pp. 375, 377.

§ Castañeda's Relations, Ternaux Compans, p. 195.

tude 40° north; and to a still larger river further on (probably the Missouri)—makes it exceedingly probable that he reached the fortieth degree of latitude, or what is now the boundary between the States of Kansas and Nebraska, well on towards the Missouri River; and in this region I have terminated his explorations north on the accompanying map.*

In regard to the *return* route of the army of Coronado, which he dispatched to Tignex before he reached Quivira, it is expressly mentioned that they passed by some salt ponds, and, as I believe they are only to be found in that region of country between the Canadian and Arkansas Rivers, on the Little Arkansas River, a tributary of the latter, in about latitude 37°, and longitude 99°, I have located this route as passing by these ponds, with some probability of its being correct.†

Another point of the return route of the army was where it struck the Rio Cicuyé, about thirty leagues below the bridge, where it had crossed it on their outward march.‡

Besides the provinces I have endeavored to locate there were a number, as I have already stated, visited by Coronado, or his officers, which were situated on the Rio Tiguex, (Rio Grande,) or some of its tributaries, as follows: Quirix, containing seven villages; in the Snow Mountains, seven; Ximena, three; Chea, one; Hemes, seven; Aguas Calientes, three; Yuque-yunque of the mountain, six; Valladolid or Braba, one; Tutahaco, eight.

Quirix was unquestionably *San Phelipe de Queres* of the present day; Chea, *Silla;* Hemes, *Hemez;* Aguas Calientes, *the ruins which I have seen at Ojos Calientes,* twelve miles above Hemez, on the Rio de Hemez; and Braba, *Taos.* The situation of all the places named accord so well with that given by Castañeda as to leave but little doubt that they are identical.

In addition, in relation to Braba, Castañeda states that it was the last town on the Rio Tiguex, north, and was "built on the two banks of a stream which was crossed by bridges built of nicely-squared pine timber." Gregg, speaking of Taos, which is the last pueblo on the Rio Grande north of Santa Fé, says: "There still exists a pueblo of Taos, composed for the most part of but two edifices of very singular construction, on each side of a creek, and formerly communicating by a bridge. The base story, near 400 feet long and 150 wide, is divided into numerous apartments, upon which other tiers of rooms are built, one above another, forming a pyramidal pile of fifty or sixty feet high, and comprising some six or eight stories."§ The identity, therefore, of the two places I think certain.

All the vilages along the Rio de Tiguex, (Rio Grande,) explored by Castañeda, were included in a district thirty leagues (102 miles) broad and one hundred and thirty (442 miles) long.

Castañeda, speaking of the origin of the people who inhabited these regions, says: "This circumstance, the customs and form of government

* This hypothesis is also strengthened by the fact that the Turk who guided Coronado stated that he was "a native of the country on the side of Florida," that is, toward the east from the Rio Tiguex, (Rio Grande,) in the valley of which he was at that time; that in his country was "a river two leagues broad," &c.; and that when he reached Quivira he told the Spaniards "that his country was still beyond that." (See Castañeda's Relations, Ternaux Compans, pp. 72, 77, 131.)

† See ante, p. 40.

‡ Between the outward and return route the Canadian River is deeply cañoned for fifty miles, which doubtless necessitated the army on its return cither to cross it where it did when going to Quivira, or at least fifty miles below that point; and doing the latter, it naturally struck the Pecos proportionally lower down from the bridge.

§ Gregg's Commerce of the Prairies, 2d ed., vol. ii, p. 277.

of these nations, which are so entirely different from those of all the other nations we have found up to the present time, prove that they came from the region of the Great India, whose coasts touch those of this country on the west. They may have approached by following the course of the river after crossing the mountains, and may have there fixed themselves in the locations that seemed most advantageous to them. As they multiplied they built other villages along the banks, until the stream failed them by plunging into the earth. When it reappears it flows toward Florida. It is said that there are other villages on the banks of this river, but we did not visit them, preferring, according to the Turk's advice, to cross the mountains to its source. I believe that great riches would be found in the country whence these Indians came. According to the route they followed they must have come from the extremity of the Eastern India, and from a very unknown region, which, according to the conformation of the coast, would be situated far in the interior of the land betwixt China and Norway. There must, in fact, be an immense distance from one sea to the other, according to the form of the coast as it has been discovered by Captain Villalobos, who took that direction in seeking for China. The same occurs when we follow the coast of Florida; it always approaches Norway up to the point where the country ' des baccalaos,' or codfish, is obtained."*

The foregoing reflections seem crude to us who are better informed with regard to the geography of the earth's surface; but when we consider that in the days of Castañeda the whole of that portion of the continent lying east of the Rio Grande was called Florida, and but little, if anything, was known of the exact relations of the northern part of our continent with the other portions of the world, they do not appear irrelevant.

In conclusion, I think it proper to observe that the "Relations" of Coronado, Castañeda, Jaramillo, and Alarcon, though somewhat vague in style, and therefore requiring a great deal of study to comprehend their meaning with certainty, are nevertheless written in a straight-forward, natural manner, and are manifestly entitled to credence whenever they describe what came under their observation. When, however, they describe the tales of others their narratives partake the character of the marvelous; but, even then, if we carry along with us the idea that they do not mean to deceive, but only to give expression to what might possibly be true—but which they do not assert to be so—their narratives must be regarded not only as truthful, but as meritorious, and eminently deserving of careful study and reflection.

---

* Castañeda's Relations, Ternaux Compans, pp. 183, 184.